WHEN THE LADY TAKES A LOVER

JESSIE CLEVER

SOMEDAY LADY PUBLISHING, LLC.

WHEN THE LADY TAKES A LOVER

Published by Someday Lady Publishing, LLC

Copyright © 2022 by Jessica McQuaid

All rights reserved.

This book is a work of fiction. Any references to historical events, real people, or real places are used fictitiously. Other names, characters, places and events are products of the author's imagination, and any resemblances to actual events or places or persons, living or dead, is entirely coincidental.

ISBN-13: 978-1-7372120-6-5

Cover Design by EDH Professionals

Edited by Judy Roth

For Kate

1

It was while she was drowning that she realized how much she hated Hawkins Savage, the Earl of Stonegate. Because just then, confronted with imminent death, she knew she'd rather die than face a lifetime of having to be grateful to the man for saving her.

But as her mouth and nose were full of water, she could not voice these concerns as he seemed to do little more than pluck her from the water. She heaved as soon as her head was free of the pond, her body rejecting the liquid as she struggled to draw a breath. It did little good.

The storm that had caused her current predicament had strengthened in the few seconds she had been in the water, and when she opened her mouth to suck in air, a gust of wind shot more water into it. She choked and coughed, spluttering to catch her breath as Hawk set her down on the bank, her feet slipping in the mud that had caused her perilous spill into the water feature in the first place.

He didn't relinquish his hold on her as she stood on unsteady feet, but worse, she gripped the front of his shirt as though it held her to this earth.

It was only then she realized how terrified she was. Still. The memory of the water closing over her was just as fresh as when it was happening seconds earlier. Only now, her traitorous brain wondered what would have happened had Hawk not seen her deadly plunge.

She'd slipped sideways into the pond, and her skirts had tangled about her legs. She was disoriented and trapped and would have drowned in four feet of water had he not seen her and plucked her from danger.

Vaguely she wondered what Hawk was even doing there, out in the storm. She had been caught in it on her way back to the house after touring the gardens with the rest of the house-party guests, traipsing after an overeager Lady Sherrill, Hawk's grandmother. She hadn't wanted to leave the house in the first place, wishing to stay where she could keep an eye on her brother and Hawk. But Audrey had insisted, and so they had gone.

Oh God, Audrey. Her cousin was still out there somewhere in the storm.

With the battering rush of wind and rain, she couldn't be sure, but it sounded like Hawk swore then, a guttural sound that cut through the disturbance around her. She'd never heard Hawk swear. His choice of weapon against her was always flattery and teasing.

She blamed this momentary confusion for what happened next. Hawk picked her up unceremoniously and strode in the direction of the house, his long legs devouring the distance and the stairs up to the terrace as if it were little more than a stroll in the gardens. She didn't even protest, and blast if she didn't hang on to the man like some simpering debutante.

She was just lucky she had fallen into the ornamental pond by the rose bushes and not the trout pond they had passed earlier. Her stomach heaved at the idea of fish getting caught in her skirts, and she worried she might spew more than water. But as she peeked a glance at Hawk's hard face, she wondered if that would really be so terrible. After all, he would likely take a direct hit.

They broke through the doors that led into the drawing rooms from the gardens, and without waiting, he simply dropped her. She crashed to the floor in a sodden heap, her legs crumpling beneath her. She didn't have time to gather a sense of herself before Hawk gripped her arm and hauled her upright.

"What on earth were you thinking? You could have been killed." He didn't raise his voice.

He never did in their altercations, and she wondered if it were that she hated most about him. His cool reserve and steady temper while she felt the need to rage at the mere sight of him. That was likely why the maybe curse word in the garden had been so unsettling.

"I was trying to be a considerate guest and take in your grandmother's gardens when she wished to show them off." Her throat was raw, but she managed the words. She thought she wouldn't be heard, but the sudden quiet of the drawing room was disconcerting.

She looked about her, at the detritus the guests had left behind mere hours earlier. They had arrived at Stonegate Manor only that morning for the house party her brother, Philip, insisted on attending, and upon arriving, she had discovered the estate already teeming with guests and potential danger for Philip.

Remembering this replaced her fright of nearly drowning with the all too familiar tension when she thought of her brother and what might have happened to him. Her eyes settled back on Hawk, and strength seemed to surge through her veins just at the sight of him, though some, like her cousin Audrey, might call it anger.

"I wouldn't even be here if it weren't for you," she said, taking a step closer to him.

His eyes narrowed. "Is that how you think of it?"

She pointed to the gardens beyond the terrace doors. "I wouldn't need to watch Philip if you didn't insist on corrupting him." She poked him childishly in the chest before shoving her sodden hair from her face. Her fingers caught in something, and she pulled her hand away to find a green bit of flora attached to her fingers. She shook her hand furiously, her stomaching tightening at the reminder of her ordeal.

"Philip is a grown man. He doesn't need your nannying."

She forgot the bit of flotsam immediately. "Nannying? I'm saving him from utter disaster." She came closer, coming up on her toes this time to draw her face closer to his. "You've already proven that it's required." She spat the accusation and readied herself for his rebuttal when his face changed.

She stilled, and it was as though the entire room around them—no, the entire manor house—stilled as well, and the world shrank to just the two of them, standing there, soaking wet and nearly toe to toe.

For one blessed moment, she thought he was going to kiss her.

And several things happened inside of her at once.

Her stomach flipped with the ever-present worry something might be slipping just out of her control, sending the last of her nerves fleeing. Her mind scrambled to mush, and finally the only thing it could produce was the image of her mother, so many years ago now, her face streaked with tears. It was as though Caroline were seeing it for the first time, and the sight of it had her rearing back, her legs vibrating with the need to put space between her and Hawk, and when that space was finally achieved, her mind cleared and with it came the absurdity of what she had thought and done.

This was Hawk. She was not in danger of being kissed by Hawk. He would never...

She lifted her gaze to his, feeling her frayed nerves wobble to life as if prepared once more to face what might be coming. But Hawk hadn't moved. He still stood where he was, his gaze narrowed and intense and focused on her.

She swallowed, the chaos of the last few minutes quieting enough for her to take him in.

He wore the same stark clothing he had been wearing earlier, and the unrelenting black she had always thought macabre appeared dangerous now. His cravat had loosened, and the wind and rain had disheveled his close-cropped russet hair. The shoulders of his jacket were soaked, and the front of his shirt showed the imprint of...her. He flexed his hands into fists and back open as if working to control his anger, and the complete image was too much.

While seconds ago she was sure he was going to kiss her, now she was certain of something far worse.

Desire.

Her body pulsed with it as she studied him.

She swallowed and turned away, shoving her hair from her face again as she attempted to pull in a steady breath to calm her nerves.

She wasn't attracted to Hawk. She simply wasn't. It was just the peril of the moment that had scattered her senses. When she turned around, everything would be set to rights.

She squared her shoulders and turned, her chin going up to resume their confrontation.

But he had moved while she had been turned, and suddenly he was closer than she had anticipated. He was far *too* close really, and she put up a hand.

"Audrey is still out there. I must—"

"Dash has gone to find her."

Dash? Well, that was interesting.

She opened her mouth to object but—

He picked her up.

Horribly, she let him.

Her arms flew around his neck to hold on.

"Where are you taking me?" she managed even as he reached the stairs.

Surely he wouldn't attempt to carry her up them.

He did.

Her lips snapped shut as she took in the tautness of his jaw, the focused intensity of his gaze.

She had never seen him like this. She had seen him annoyed, angry, frustrated, and mocking, but this...well, she would wager he looked frightened, which made little sense. What had Hawkins Savage, the Earl of Stonegate, have to be frightened of?

They gained the upper floor, and he turned, striding down the length of it without comment. Her arms tightened reflexively around him.

He was taking her to her rooms.

"Hawk," she tried for a measured tone. "Hawk, you must put me down. We can't be seen—"

"There's no one in the house to see us." The words were nearly growled, and she didn't know if he meant them as a threat or comfort.

Her stomach turned again, but it wasn't tension this time that had it coiling. It was anticipation.

She didn't speak again until they reached her rooms,

and he boorishly kicked open the door to her rooms. The way he dropped her once again should have extinguished any romantic notions she might have held, and yet there was something about the tension radiating from his body that told her something wasn't as it always had been.

She plucked at her wet skirts as she straightened, attempting to appear presentable for a reason she couldn't fathom. Hawk strode away from her in the direction of her bedchamber. Her eyes widened as she watched him go, and it was several seconds before she realized she should stop him.

"Hawk?" she called after him as she scrambled across the sitting room that opened onto the bedchamber.

She had wondered why she had been given such a generous accommodation as she was no one of rank, being only the daughter of a marquess. Perhaps it was because she was Philip's sister. Hawk's grandmother might have seen her as an honored guest as she was family to Hawk's oldest and dearest friend.

She gritted her teeth at the thought, but she had more pressing matters to attend. She sailed into her bedchamber just as Hawk wrenched open the doors of her armoire.

She pushed in front of him, effectively closing the doors and shielding her private things from his prying eyes.

"Excuse me." She announced each word individually to give them more weight. "What are you doing?"

He eyed her. "You need to change into dry clothes before you catch a chill."

Her eyes widened. She couldn't have stopped them. "Are you concerned for my wellbeing?"

He leaned close, and she could see the gold specks in his brown eyes. "I'm concerned for my best friend's sister's wellbeing. What do you take me for? A brute?"

She couldn't help the eyebrow that went up at this. "I take you for many things. A brute being one of the milder ones."

He growled, the sound muted by his clenched teeth. "Will you simply find something dry to put on? I don't want Philip to think I kept you from seeing to your health."

She crossed her arms over her chest. "My health is just fine. I want to know why you think you have the right—"

"Stop."

She started so suddenly her head bounced against the armoire behind her. Never before in the more than ten years she'd known Hawk had she heard him bellow a word the way he did then.

He had turned when he'd spoken, and his back was to her now. She noted the rigid line of his shoulder, the taut outline of the muscles of his back. Her heart thudded in her chest as a shiver passed cleanly down her body.

Had she finally gone too far? Had she finally pushed him further than she had ought?

She wanted to ask him. She wanted to apologize, which was ridiculous. He didn't deserve her apology. But there was something about the way he stood. It appeared almost as if he were trying to hold himself together.

She reached up before she knew she was going to, and her hand hung suspended in the air before her as she almost—*almost*—touched him.

She knew what she would find. Hard muscle and heat. She knew it without knowing how, and her stomach rolled, her emotions mixing with the ever-present tension until she didn't know what to feel.

It all fell away even as she tried to sift through it, and there was nothing left but the need to touch him. At first she wasn't sure if she had touched him or not because her hand hardly moved. She wanted to feel that rush of heat from him, stroke the hard muscles she knew were there, but none of that happened.

Because just as she made contact, he whirled about and swept her into his arms, pressing her back against the armoire, his hard body pinning her there as his lips descended on hers in a hot, tumultuous kiss.

A sound she had never made before stuck in her throat, and the breath seized in her lungs, but before she could take stock of it, her body took over where her mind failed. Her arms went around him, pulling him solidly against her as she tilted her head, inviting him to deepen the kiss.

He did, sweeping his tongue along the seam of her lips before plunging it inside. Heat flooded her, and the tension that never seemed to go away suddenly dispersed. She pictured it floating away from her body as there was no longer room for it. Not with the things he was doing to her, the things he was making her feel.

His hands swept down the sides of her body, and she shivered, wanting him to touch her everywhere. Had she been thinking clearly, she would have been shocked by the wantonness of her thoughts, let alone that she was having them for Hawk.

But that was just it. She wasn't thinking. She was feeling and responding, and her body sang with a sudden freedom it had never known.

The invisible weight she had carried since she witnessed her mother's destruction, since Philip's near ruin, evaporated, and if not gone, at least relieved for the time being, and suddenly she didn't want Hawk to stop.

But as soon as she thought it, he did.

He wrenched away from her, putting deliberate space

between them as he sucked in a breath and pushed his hands through his hair.

"Caroline, we can't do this." He shook his head. "*I* can't do this. I can't do this to Philip."

And like a spell being broken, the tension settled itself once more on her shoulders at the sound of her brother's name spoken from Hawkins Savage's lips.

And once more, she remembered how much she hated this man.

HE KNEW AS SOON as the words left his lips that he shouldn't have spoken them.

Their emotions were too high and volatile, the tension raw and real. Speaking Philip's name was like throwing fuel on a barn fire.

He ran his hands through his hair and turned away, stifling a curse. He braced himself for the attack he knew was coming. He drew a breath and held it, counted to ten, willed himself to find calm.

Because no matter what she accused him of he could not defend himself.

"Philip? You would speak of Philip as if you had some kind of regard for him?"

He gritted his teeth. Philip might have been her brother, but he was Hawk's oldest and dearest friend. Thinking he held the man in some kind of regard was appallingly insufficient. Hawk would give his life for Philip. He cringed at the image, knowing how little it meant considering what was only mere weeks away now.

He turned back to her. "I hold Philip in the highest regard," he said uselessly.

It didn't matter what he said. He had come to learn that in the five years since she'd first laid blame at his feet.

"Is that what you told him when you suggested his dalliance with Lady Winnaretta?"

He admired many things about Lady Caroline Hodge. Her heart-shaped face, her thick, golden hair, her stunningly blue eyes, and her body. Yes, he would admit he loved her body. She was on the shorter side, but she made up for it in ample curves.

But the thing he loved most about her was her forthrightness.

Her directness spoke of courage he saw lacking in many of the men who had fought beside him on the continent. She never held back what she was thinking even when her place and sex would suggest she keep her mouth shut.

Her honesty was just so damn appealing.

"I suggested his dalliance with Lady Winnaretta?" He raised an eyebrow. "Do you know in five years I don't believe you've ever accused me of orchestrating their encounter."

"Then I apologize for the oversight." She crossed her arms over her stomach, water dripping from the sleeves of her gown.

He glanced down to see the puddle forming beneath her on the floor and mentally cursed himself for the distraction.

"Apology accepted." He held up both hands as she opened her mouth for what he knew would be a scathing retort. "As invigorating as this discussion is sure to be, I must insist on you changing before we continue." He backed to the door of the bedchamber before she could argue. "I will happily wait in the sitting room for the dressing down I'm sure you'd like to give me."

He backed through the door and snapped it shut behind

him, pressing his forehead to the wood as he sucked in a much-needed, calming breath.

She could have drowned.

The thought alone was enough to turn his blood cold even now that the danger had passed. If he, Philip, and their friend Dash hadn't decided to go after the house-party guests in the gardens when the storm rolled in, he would not have seen Caroline tumble into the pond. She didn't surface in the ten seconds it had taken him to reach her, and he knew had he not been there to pull her free, her restrictive garments would have meant her doom.

He pushed away from the door, yanking at his sodden jacket until he could rip his arms free. He tossed the garment aside carelessly and paced the length of the room, drawing steady breaths as he willed his racing heart to settle.

He had kissed her.

He had been so careful in the last few years not to act on his attraction for her. It would have been simple enough to think she was too young and too full of hate and blame for him and his role in the near scandal her brother's broken engagement had caused. He had often wondered what might have happened had Philip told her the truth, but Philip never had. He was in the same predicament as Hawk. It wasn't their secret to tell.

It was Lady Winnaretta's secret.

It was this that had kept him from spilling the truth five years ago. He wasn't sure which was worse. Knowing the truth or knowing the truth in the face of Caroline's disdain.

Philip was nothing more than the victim of a broken engagement. Thankfully it had been the chatter of the ballroom for all of a season and easily forgotten. Lady Winnaretta had fared far worse, and yet Caroline never seemed to speak her name. It was he who remained the target of her displeasure, and he'd never been able to reason why.

Philip's reputation was firmly intact. Lady Winnaretta had vanished from society. But Caroline still hated him, and he had never understood it.

The door to the bedchamber opened long before he expected it to, and he halted in his pacing to turn. She strode into the room, her dressing gown flapping about her legs.

Her bare legs.

Oh. Dear. Jesus.

She hadn't dressed. From what he could see, she'd shed her sodden garments to replace them with nothing more than her dressing gown. He could even see her toes. Her precious, little toes as they dug into the carpet.

He immediately suspected her actions were deliberate. He'd given away too much by kissing her, and now she was determined to make him ache. But the fire in her eyes suggested something else entirely.

"I was not apologizing to you, Stonegate, and you know it. You of all people should recognize sarcasm."

Her hair was wet and loose around her shoulders, and he had the absurd urge to push her into a chair so he could brush it out. Preferably in front of a crackling fire with wine before he drew her down to the rug on the hearth and made love to her.

He whirled away from her and resumed his pacing, gritting his teeth so hard he feared he'd crack a molar.

What had happened to him? He had so carefully guarded his desire for her for three long, painful years, but now it seemed the dam had broken.

It was because of what had happened. It was the sudden

spike of fear that had shot through him at the sight of her disappearing through the water, the blueness of her lips when he'd pulled her free, the way she'd shivered uncontrollably without seeming to notice.

That was all.

It was just the heightened circumstances that had tested his resolve. He had loved her since the moment he laid eyes on her at her coming out ball three years ago, and he had never broken once. Surely it was just the stress of the day.

He turned back to her. "You did not do as I asked." He pointed to her dressing gown. "That is hardly enough to prevent a chill. Surely you have some...stockings." It took every fiber of his focus to find a suitable word.

She placed her fists on her hips. "My stockings are irrelevant at the moment."

Heat flooded her cheeks, and he thought she must have realized the inappropriateness of what she'd said. But then only minutes ago, she had been wrapped around him in an embrace full of far more sensuality than wool stockings could ever hope to muster.

"Be that as it may, I will not be responsible should you fall ill." He pointed at the bedchamber behind her. "Go dress."

"Do not tell me what to do."

He leaned down. "I will tell you what to do when it's for your own good."

"Just as you helped my brother?"

"I didn't—" He stopped so abruptly he almost bit his tongue.

He couldn't tell her the truth.

"Philip became acquainted with Lady Winnaretta through his own means. I had nothing to do with the encounter."

Her eyes narrowed. "But it was you who enjoyed the company of women. Surely Philip's own tastes were influenced. I am aware of your reputation, Lord Stonegate."

He straightened. "My what?"

She hesitated. "Your reputation." The words were not as strong now.

He crossed his arms over his chest. "I wasn't aware I had a reputation, Lady Caroline." He raised an eyebrow to prod her into saying more.

She hesitated again, and he couldn't help but enjoy it. It wasn't often he managed to upset her course. Upset, yes. But distract her from her goal? That was rare indeed, and he wished to savor it.

It was some moments before she spoke, and when she did, her voice was desperate. "You danced with Lady Diana. Twice."

He dropped his arms and shook his head. "Lady Diana is the daughter of a dear friend of my grandmother's. She had expressed to Grandmother her disappointment in the lack of attention Lady Diana was receiving this season, and I offered to help."

Caroline's lips parted, and she blinked furiously.

He attempted to hold back the smile, but the moment was too rich. "Grandmother informed me just yesterday that Lady Diana has received three proposals of marriage. One from a duke."

Caroline snapped her mouth shut as she seemed to consider if he were telling the truth. "But I—"

"But you wish for me to play the villain, and the truth of it is I am simply not one."

"But you are." She spoke the words succinctly and vehemently, and he was sure she absolutely believed them.

It was at moments like this when it was easier to

pretend. To forget the way the mere sight of her made him smile. To forget the way he watched for her to enter a crowded ballroom. To forget the way her scent—roses and fresh air—seemed to curl inside of him and linger whenever she was near.

She truly did believe him a villain, and there was nothing he could do to correct her thinking.

Besides, it was better this way. His thirtieth birthday loomed on the horizon, a mere six weeks away, and then it would all be over. None of this would matter.

It wouldn't matter.

None of this would.

Caroline's disdain for him. Philip's near scandal.

None of it.

Because after he turned thirty...

He wasn't sure when he had stopped seeing past his thirtieth birthday. Perhaps it was when he became aware of the fact that he was closing in on the age his father had been when he'd died. Hawk somehow couldn't fathom how he could live to be older than his own father, and when the realization had occurred to him, everything had stopped.

The years past his thirtieth birthday vanished, and he was seized with an inevitableness.

He would never see thirty-one. He couldn't. He couldn't age further than his own father. It just wasn't possible. He pictured his thirtieth birthday like a clock ticking down, and soon it would all be over. He didn't how it would happen, and he couldn't recall when the sensation had taken hold of him. He only knew one thing for certain. He would stop existing the moment he turned thirty.

It didn't matter if Caroline believed him to be a villain because in only a matter of weeks his life would cease to matter.

All of it would cease to matter.

He was struck in that moment by the intensity of her beauty. She was so, so beautiful it hurt him. Physically.

He would never have her. Not because she believed the worst of him, and he could never tell her the truth. But because fate had dealt him a blow from which he could never recover. He stood before the woman he wanted to spend the rest of his life with, and his life was made up of only a few, short remaining weeks, and because of that, he would never pursue her.

Only a few weeks more and then it would be over. It had to be. Because nothing else made sense.

He studied her a moment longer before making up his mind.

He would never have her, but that didn't mean he couldn't steal a taste of her.

He knew it was only because he surprised her that he was able to pull her into his embrace once more, to crush his lips to hers.

Had she resisted even the slightest bit, he would have stopped immediately. But she didn't.

Instead she wrapped herself completely around him, her arms about his neck, her leg coming up to wrap around his calf. Her lips were hot and frantic against his, and then —dear God, her hands were in his hair, pinning him to her.

He could feel every one of her curves through the thin fabric of her dressing gown, and all at once, he *ached* for her.

He wanted Caroline Hodge like he had never wanted anything before, and she hated him with a passion that held no equal.

So, he let her go and left the room.

2

S he had thought when she returned to London everything would go back to normal. She could forget about what had happened at Stonegate Manor. She would forget that she had kissed Hawk. It would be easy to forget. Once she had some distance, she would remember what he had done to her brother, and her determination to protect Philip from Hawk's devious ways would be renewed.

But as she sat alone at the breakfast table that morning, the softly falling rain the only sound accompanying the clink of her fork against her plate, she didn't feel so convinced.

The truth of it was she was rather tired.

Since she had witnessed the mental and emotional destruction of her mother at the hands of her father, Caroline had done everything she could to control the outcome of her life because if she didn't, she would end up like her mother.

So, when she saw the same destruction happening in

her brother's life, her instincts had kicked in, and her feud with Hawk had begun.

Only now...

She was tired of fighting him off. She was tired of protecting Philip. She was tired of the tension that radiated through her body as she held on to everything.

And kissing Hawk had given her a glimpse of something else, something she hadn't known existed.

The freedom of letting go.

It was like a drug. The memory of its lightness tantalizing her, beckoning her, calling for her to find more of it. With Hawk.

She set down her fork, her eggs untouched on her plate except for the channels she had carved mindlessly through them.

Hawk's body had been so hard pressed against hers. She hadn't known it would feel like that. To be pressed against someone. To be pressed against Hawk. To feel his heat even through the damp of their clothes. The fright of her near drowning had vanished the moment he'd touched her, and she'd never known anything to have such power.

And his kiss.

She raised a hand to her lips, swearing she could feel the memory of his kiss as though it were happening still. It didn't make sense. How could it feel so good?

Her mind flashed to that night so many years ago now. Her mother's face streaked with tears, her words intelligible except for the accusations she'd flung at Caroline's father. Caroline had seen what love did to people, and she dropped her hand to her lap.

She had to stop thinking this way. The only thing to be done was to keep Philip safe. She couldn't let him be almost ruined again. She couldn't let herself fall under Hawk's spell.

She put her napkin on the table, prepared to stand when faintly she heard the front door open and close down the hall. There were only a handful of people that would come through the front door without knocking first.

Her skin tingled, and her breath hitched before the thought fully formed in her mind.

Hawk had come to see her.

No, he would be coming to see Philip. God, why was this happening to her?

When her hopes fell at the sight of Audrey tripping through the door seconds later, she instantly hated herself for her wandering, hopeful thoughts.

But at the sight of Audrey's bright, smiling face, Caroline forgot all about Hawk.

"What's happened?" Caroline breathed before Audrey could say anything.

Her cousin came around the table as Caroline slowly stood, anticipation gathering along her shoulders in tense worry, that feeling of losing control sneaking up behind her.

Audrey seized Caroline's hands, her cheeks bright with color and her eyes—her eyes shone. Almost as if she were...

Caroline shook her head. It couldn't be possible. "Audrey, what it is?"

"I'm getting married," Audrey whispered, her head shaking slightly as well, as if she couldn't believe her own words. "Dash and I are to be wed."

The earth fell out beneath Caroline's feet. That was the only thing that could explain how her stomach dropped at the announcement. For she couldn't have felt betrayal by her cousin. How unfair would that be? Audrey was a confirmed wallflower. The fact that she should be marrying an earl—an earl Caroline was sure Audrey loved—was a miracle and blessing.

So why did it feel like Audrey had forsaken her?

Her sense of control slipped a little more.

Too late Caroline remembered to smile. "Oh, Audrey, that's wonderful." Even she could hear the lack of excitement in her voice.

Audrey's smile faded. "Caroline, what is it?"

Audrey was not one to mince words, but Caroline shook her head. "It's nothing. It's just—" She let out a blast of air with a shaky laugh. "Oh Audrey, it was just a shock."

She pulled her hands free to throw her arms around her cousin to hide the emotions she tried to wrangle in place before they showed on her face.

Audrey was getting married.

Tears stung unexpectedly at the backs of her eyes, and fear gripped her chest until she thought she couldn't breathe. She blinked rapidly, tightening her hold on Audrey, buying herself much-needed time.

Audrey was getting married.

Caroline's Audrey.

Audrey deserved happiness. Her cousin was everything wonderful about the world, and to see her with Dash was... heartbreaking. What if Dash did to Audrey what Caroline's father had done to her mother?

Caroline squeezed her eyes shut tight, hating herself for thinking that way. She couldn't keep Audrey to herself, standing at the edges of ballrooms forever. Audrey deserved more, and Caroline could only pray Dash was worthy of her.

It was just that it was all too much, and that whirling empty feeling inside of her was growing, threatening to consume her. The world kept spinning out from under her feet, and she couldn't chase it.

Audrey would marry, and Caroline had kissed Hawk.

Hawk.

All at once she realized she couldn't breathe. There was no air in the breakfast room, and the skin along her arms felt alive, as if hundreds of critters crawled along them.

She had to get out of there.

But she couldn't. Audrey had come to her. To share her news. News about which she was so excited.

Despair filled Caroline, and she sucked in a breath, squared her shoulders, and pulled back, forcing a smile to her lips.

"Audrey, that is truly wonderful."

Audrey's smile faded slowly before she pulled Caroline's arm through hers. "Did you know it's a beautiful morning? I think a walk in the garden is called for."

Caroline knew perfectly well it was raining, but Audrey didn't take her into the foyer to gather a cloak. She turned Caroline in the direction of the terrace doors off the breakfast room without giving her a moment to argue, and Caroline let herself be led like a child, her chest tight, her arms tingling.

The misty cold air of the garden hit her like a blast of life, and she sucked in a breath as if it were her first. The rain had subsided to a light drizzle, and it was invigorating against her cheeks and forehead. She lifted her face to the gray sky, the tension in her shoulders slipping away.

She tugged on Audrey's arm. "Thank you," she whispered.

Audrey only smiled and turned her attention to the dewy hedges. "You know a wedding takes time to plan, and I don't wish to embark on such an endeavor with my mother. I had hoped you would help me." She stopped at the edge of the stone path that led into the gardens and turned to Caroline. "You know I haven't the faintest idea of what is required of a bride."

Caroline snorted a laugh. "And I do?"

"Not at all. That's what should make this so fun. We'll drive my mother mad."

They both laughed then, and Caroline felt her sense of control begin to piece itself back together. She pulled Audrey close for another hug.

"I'm sorry, cousin," she whispered. "You know..." She let her voice trail off.

She didn't know what it was that gripped her sometimes, what made her feel like she was losing control, but she knew Audrey understood without saying the words.

"I know," Audrey whispered with a squeeze. This time when she stepped back, her cousin's look was understanding. "I know this must come as a shock to you. It's still very much a shock to me." Her smile was self-deprecating before she sobered. "But you know, not all marriages are like the one your mother and father have." Audrey looked askance, as though peering internally. "Come to that, not all marriages are like my own parents'." She laughed now, wholeheartedly, and shook her head. "I really hope you can understand that and not worry so much."

Caroline's only response was to frown ponderously.

Audrey pursed her lips before saying, "And when are you going to tell me what happened at the house party?"

Caroline's lips parted. "What do you mean?"

The mist hung around them, and it was as though they were suspended in their own world, far away from everything else. It was safe here, just the two of them. And yet Caroline felt her throat closing.

"Because the look you've had on your face since we

returned is the same one I wore after my first encounter with Dash."

Caroline snapped her mouth shut. Audrey had encountered Dash in a rather bold embrace in a cloakroom and had shared every scandalous detail with Caroline.

Caroline shook her head. "It's nothing like that."

"It's exactly like that. So why don't you tell me—"

"It's not, Audrey. I promise. It's—"

Audrey waved away her concerns. "There's nothing permanent from one little encounter. You know how long it took for me and Dash to—"

"I kissed Hawk." She blurted out the words so quickly, she nearly bit her own tongue.

Audrey's words died on her parted lips, and they stared at one another for several heartbeats.

Audrey finally said, "Hawk? As in your archenemy Hawk?"

Caroline could only nod frantically as she felt her newly regained control slipping.

Audrey took her arm again and propelled her down the stone path between the hedges. They were silent for several paces before Audrey stopped.

"Hawk? Hawkins Savage? You kissed him?" Audrey's eyes were wide and wondering.

"I think we kissed each other."

Audrey blinked and kept walking, her hand seeming to unconsciously pat Caroline's arm.

Again, Audrey stopped. "But you hate him. He torments you."

"I know. I don't know what happened." Caroline despised how unsteady her voice was. "The storm came up, and I fell into that pond, and Hawk was there, and—" She shrugged, unable to finish the story.

Audrey nodded and kept nodding. "All right. That's fine. It was unusual circumstances. Tension was high, I'm sure. You were probably frightened, and Hawk was being overly protective. You might be the thorn in his side, but you're still his best friend's little sister. It was just instinctual. That's all."

"I think I want him to kiss me again." Caroline pressed her lips together, afraid more betraying words would slip through.

"Oh dear," Audrey said and stopped nodding as she started blinking furiously. She shook her head harshly and grabbed Caroline by the shoulders. "Caroline, you're worried over nothing. Hawk is an earl and a gentleman. You could choose a worse man over whom to have such desires. I really think—"

Caroline latched onto Audrey's arms. "But that's just it. I don't want—" She snapped her mouth shut.

She had never told anyone about this. Not even Audrey. She had never spoken of what she had seen that night. Audrey knew Caroline saw her parents' marriage as evidence of the state of most society marriages, but Caroline had never spoken of the utter destruction she had seen. The same destruction Caroline swore to never let happen to her.

Audrey's grip softened. "I know, Caroline. I know you don't wish for such attachment, but perhaps you could see this as an opportunity to explore an alternative. Like I said, one encounter won't dictate the rest of your life."

Attachment. Audrey was speaking of marriage. The formality of it. But it wasn't that which Caroline feared.

It was the power someone could have over her if she gave them her affection.

But perhaps there was something else in what Audrey said.

She studied her cousin. Audrey had kissed Dash in a

cloakroom, passionately by her cousin's retelling of the event. Perhaps what happened at the house party was her own version of that. An exploration, a discovery. It didn't mean something permanent.

But did it mean she could keep exploring without putting her heart in danger?

Part of her wished she could, a very secret, small part of her. The same part of her that longed to live without the ever-present worry that seemed to cling to her like a veil.

"Perhaps you're right," she said now and pulled Audrey's arm through hers and steered her back toward the house.

"Now tell me what happened. The last I knew you were never going to speak to Dash again."

Audrey related the story of her engagement as they made their way back to the house, and while Caroline listened, she couldn't stop her mind from wandering.

Maybe Audrey was right. Maybe it wouldn't change her life if she were to explore her feelings for Hawk. Everything was changing around her, and perhaps if she changed a little with it, it wouldn't seem so jarring and sudden.

But even as she tried to convince herself of it, it still felt as though the earth was no longer solid beneath her feet. She knew what happened when things changed, when people acted on emotions.

And nothing good could ever come of it.

When they reached the breakfast room again, Caroline had convinced herself that she had been right in the first place. It was best to avoid such volatility as emotions conjured. Besides, she had Audrey's wedding to distract her. She promised to go to Dartford House the next day to begin planning.

Audrey gave her one more squeeze before turning to the door. "I'm off to see Grandmother Regina and tell her the news." She hesitated at the door, her slight overbite worrying her lower lip. "Caroline, do you think Grandmother Regina had anything to do with Dash and I?"

Caroline tilted her head, considering. "What do you mean?"

Audrey shrugged. "It's just that Dash and I are so well suited for one another. It seems odd that we should have..." She made a gesture then as if to encompass the entirety of her situation.

Caroline shook her head. "I'm not sure Grandmother Regina is capable of such scheming now."

Grandmother Regina had suffered a stroke some years ago, and her youngest daughter, Verity, cared for her. Such an arrangement would suggest secret matchmaking was beyond her abilities.

Audrey frowned. "I suppose you're right. It just seems odd."

Caroline shrugged. "Sometimes the best things have no explanation."

Audrey smiled. "I suppose you're right," she said and raised a hand in farewell before disappearing through the door.

Caroline sank down at the breakfast table, her untouched and now cold breakfast in front of her, wishing she believed her own words.

He had tried to stay away.

He thought if he gave the problem some distance its power would fade. He didn't care to think of her in those terms, but that's essentially what she was. He couldn't let himself fall under her spell for too many reasons. He was going to spend the morning with Philip to remind him of the importance of one of those reasons.

But he hadn't expected to run into Audrey with an expression on her face not unlike a cat who had caught a mouse.

He slipped into Mattingly House as Lady Audrey D'Arcy clearly had been slipping out, and this at first gave him pause. He couldn't recall a time when Audrey and Caroline weren't together, and the hour was still early. Surely Audrey couldn't be leaving already. It wasn't uncommon to see the cousins together at the Mattingly breakfast table long after the food had been cleared away, but that didn't seem to be the case this morning.

If the early hour and lack of Caroline weren't alarming enough, the stark look on Audrey's face when she met him on the front stoop should have been.

"Good morning, Lady Audrey," he said with a respectful tip of his chin.

It was as though it were all Audrey could do to hold back a laugh. "Hawk," she said and bid him good day, flying down the remainder of the steps and into a waiting carriage.

He paused in the foyer as the door closed behind the D'Arcy cousin, and he felt the certainty of the situation close in on him.

Caroline had told Audrey what had happened at the house party.

Had she told Philip then too?

He knew Caroline hadn't spoken to Audrey immediately upon her return because he had encountered the D'Arcy cousin several times socially since then, and she had seemed distracted, not at all intent on his immediate death for violating her precious cousin.

Now he wasn't sure what to think. Audrey's look had not

been one of murder. If anything, it was obvious she had attempted to avoid his eye. And what did that mean? He knew there was a budding relationship between Audrey and Hawk's school friend Dashiell Evers, the Earl of Amberley. Perhaps Dash had spilled some sense into Audrey's ear about Hawk's reputation.

Had Audrey then told Caroline?

He stopped abruptly in his trek down the corridor in the direction of the breakfast room, the thought upsetting what had been the natural order of things.

What if Caroline were to learn the truth of what had happened with Lady Winnaretta from someone other than him or Philip? Only Dash hadn't been there when Philip suffered the broken engagement. But it didn't truly matter anyway. The countdown to his thirtieth birthday had begun, and it was all just a matter of time.

He continued on, knowing he may stumble upon Caroline in the breakfast room, but it was the most likely place to find Philip.

Only he didn't find Philip at all.

He found Caroline instead. Like he had never seen her before.

It stopped him completely.

He had never seen Caroline appear...*forlorn.*

The word lodged uncomfortably in his chest, but he couldn't pry his eyes away from her. She sat at the table, shoulders slumped, and her eyes unfocused.

She appeared lost.

He should leave. He moved a foot as if to do just that, but then—

She released a sigh, and it was the saddest sound he had ever heard. It was like the sound a fairy's wings would make if broken or like a puppy crying from having its paw trampled.

His heart broke knowing what he was about to do.

He would engage with her once more at her disadvantage, and he felt like a scoundrel. It wasn't fair of him to do this to her, to appear when she was at her worst when he knew she'd wish to have her faculties rallied to launch some perceived battle with him.

But he couldn't leave her like that, lost and lonely at the empty breakfast table.

So instead of turning around, he walked into the breakfast room.

"Good morning, pet," he said, plastering on a smile he didn't feel.

Her head snapped up at his use of the endearment he knew she loathed, and he saw something else he hadn't expected to see that day.

For just a moment, a very brief moment, one so minuscule it could have been a flutter of his imagination, Caroline appeared eager to see him.

Only as quickly as he saw it, she hid it, along with the sadness he had so recently seen there. He noted this but kept moving across the room until he pulled out the chair next to her and sat down.

"I didn't hear the door."

He tilted his head, a smile creeping onto his lips. "Listening for me, pet?"

Her cheeks flamed. "What are you doing here?"

He felt better seeing the color flare over her pale skin, but then it only made him wonder what she would look like in the throes of passionate lovemaking. He swallowed and turned to the table, picking up an unused cup.

"Coffee?" he asked.

"I asked you a question."

He poured himself a cup of the thick, steaming liquid, having no intention at all of drinking it. "And I ignored it." He raised an eyebrow. "Not feeling peckish this morning, pet?"

Her brow folded in irritation. "My desires are no business of yours."

He nearly dropped the coffee urn, and his eyes flashed to hers. He knew she understood she'd used the absolute wrong word by the way her eyes went wide, and her lips thinned to a line.

She swallowed and turned away from him. "Philip isn't here. He's gone to look at some horseflesh with Father."

He could almost feel how much each of those words hurt for her to speak them, and he leaned back in his chair, holding the cup of coffee between both hands in a feigned pose of casualness. If Philip weren't home, Caroline was for all intents and purposes alone as her parents never bothered to see to her doings.

Hawk should have gotten the hell out of there.

But he couldn't leave her. Not like this. He had to know what had caused that look of sadness he had witnessed and if there was anything he could do to relieve it, even if it meant only serving as a momentary distraction.

"I'm sure your mother will be down shortly."

This got him the quick, cold look he knew it would. "You know perfectly well Mother never comes down to breakfast."

And that was exactly why he should have left.

He took a sip of his coffee instead, hiding a grimace at the taste. "Tell me then, pet. What has you lingering at the table in such a lonely state this morning?"

He was careful to pepper the question with words he

knew would trigger her ire. Except it seemed nothing was going to go as planned that morning because instead of the explosion he'd expected, Caroline stood and walked away from him, her back rigid and unyielding, her arms akimbo so he could only see the points of her elbows protruding from each side of her.

He set down his cup. Something was very wrong.

"Caroline." He kept his tone low and easy.

She stopped in front of the terrace doors, her shoulders stiff. The rain had picked up again, and it struck the window in a pronounced staccato. Slowly he gained his feet, but he made no advance.

After what seemed an eternity, Caroline spoke. "Audrey and Dash are to be wed."

He wasn't surprised by the news, but rather he hadn't expected it so soon.

"Dash finally convinced her of his worthiness?" He didn't know the details of their courtship, but he knew from Dash that it hadn't gone smoothly.

Caroline nodded but kept her back to him. He didn't know how as he couldn't see her face, but he sensed she was trying to hold back tears. It chipped away at what little restraint he had left.

"I suppose that's wonderful news." He took a tentative step toward her. When she didn't turn on him or bolt, he took another. "When is the fated occasion to take place?"

He kept his tone light and inviting, so when she whirled around, her eyes wet with tears, her mouth tight with fury, he wasn't entirely ready for it.

"I don't know, Hawk. I don't know anything. Why do you insist on badgering me?"

She no longer looked sad. Now she looked as though her whole world were splintering into a thousand pieces.

Don't kiss her. Don't pull her into your arms and tell her everything will be all right. Don't touch her.

But even as he told himself not to do it, his hands flexed, wanting to pull her close, to comfort her.

He licked his lips. "Caroline, I don't understand. I thought you would be happy—"

"I *am* happy." She nearly screamed the words, and the tears broke loose, cascading down her cheeks as sobs wracked her body.

He gave up and gave in, pulling her against him and wrapping both arms snuggly around her. She didn't resist. In fact, her arms went immediately around his waist, her hands pressing into his back.

He held her like that for several seconds, trying not to think about how perfectly she fit against him, how neatly her head tucked just under his chin, and worst of all, how good it felt to hold her against him.

He gritted his teeth and closed his eyes. He couldn't let this overcome him. He had to keep his senses about him. It wouldn't matter soon. Soon it would all be over. Caroline would be free of him.

The thought had his eyes opening.

Caroline would be free of him.

It should have brought him joy, but it only brought despair.

There was her scent—roses and fresh air—and he wondered if it came from her soap. But it was mixed with a dampness he thought the day might have brought. Had she been outside walking in the rain? Why?

It was none of his business. The realization was crushing, but he didn't have time to ruminate on the thought. Because just then Caroline ripped herself from his arms, accusations spewing from her lips. It was a startled moment before he realized the accusations were not being hurtled at him. She was berating herself.

"I should be happy for her, Hawk. I should be so happy for her. She deserves to be in love. She deserves happiness. She's a beautiful person, Hawk. Why am I not happy for her? Why? Why am I so...so..." Her words spluttered out then, and her eyes wandered about her as if searching for an explanation for her feelings.

He pulled her back into his arms. Tucking her into his embrace, he cupped the back of her head and held her while she cried.

"You're allowed to feel this way, Caroline. Audrey means everything to you, and now things will be different. You're allowed to feel scared and unsure. Change can be unsettling, and only time will make things better."

He was making a mess of her hair, but he didn't care. She appeared not to either as she allowed him to hold her, to massage the base of her skull.

He didn't know how long they stood like that, but eventually her tears subsided. He didn't let her go though, and she didn't push him away.

The rain fell against the terrace doors, and the house settled quietly around them.

He was filled with such a sudden lust for this kind of domesticity it frightened him.

But this wasn't meant for him. None of this was, and he eased her gently away.

When she blinked up at him, her eyelashes were heavy with tears, and her lips were parted as if a question lingered there.

He let himself cup her cheek, to stroke his thumb along the arch there.

He didn't realize he shook his head until Caroline asked, "What is it?"

He licked his lips, willing himself not to speak his thoughts, but like everything when it came to Caroline, he couldn't seem to control himself.

"The world knows of your beauty, but they can't know the half of it. They can't know how beautiful your soul is." He shook his head again. "I can't understand how it is I'm so lucky as to know all of you."

She stood there in his arms, blinking, as the realness of the moment penetrated his senses. He had overstepped. He had broken his own rules and gone too far. But her eyes, her damn eyes, had captivated him. *She* had captivated him.

He couldn't let this happen, and there was only one way to ensure it didn't.

He had to get away from her.

He eased her farther away, but he only let go of her when he was sure she was steady on her feet.

"You'll be all right, Caroline," he said. "You always are."

He left before she could say anything to make him lose the last of his resolve.

3

He had called her by her name.

She had been at a moment of such utter weakness. He could have used any one of his needling pet names for her, and it would have been met with the greatest annoying success. But he hadn't. He'd called her by her name. Her *given* name.

She sat in the Dartford House drawing room, holding a cup of rapidly cooling tea, her eyes unseeing as she replayed the scene in the breakfast room over and over again in her head.

That was not the Hawk she knew. The Hawk she knew encouraged her brother to indulge in ruinous behavior. The Hawk she knew was dangerous and corrupting.

But the Hawk who held her so tenderly was not the same man.

She didn't know what to do with this new Hawk. Audrey's words kept tumbling over and over again in her head. Had she been wrong about the man this whole time? Was there more to him that she didn't know?

She tried to focus on the rising steam from the tea, forcing order to her thoughts.

Audrey couldn't be right. Caroline had asked her brother directly the truth of the matter when he had announced his sudden engagement to Lady Winnaretta. It was obvious why her brother was forced to make such an engagement, and even at such a young age, Caroline had known the truth of it. Her brother wouldn't lie to her about how Lady Winnaretta had gotten into her predicament. Would he?

She tried to focus, pulling the memory of that long ago afternoon to the fore. Her brother had summoned the family to the drawing room. Her mother had dissolved into hysterics. Her father had mumbled incoherent noises about honor and respect. Her mother fretted that someone would count the months from wedding to the birth of the babe.

But what had struck Caroline as odd was the absence of Lady Winnaretta.

Hadn't Lady Winnaretta's future been at stake that afternoon as well?

Why hadn't she been there to defend herself?

Had she been too frightened?

Audrey was always reminding Caroline that she was stronger than some women of society. Perhaps Lady Winnaretta had been afraid to face Philip's family. But why? It was Philip who had ruined her. If anything, it should be Caroline's family who owed Lady Winnaretta an apology for Philip's behavior.

So why hadn't Lady Winnaretta been there?

Audrey might be right. Lady Winnaretta may have been reluctant to face them, ashamed of what had happened. On some level, Caroline understood this. Love was a diabolical thing, and it could cause one to make terrible decisions. This was obvious in Lady Winnaretta's case.

It was too easy to compare Caroline's own mistake to that of Lady Winnaretta. Caroline had let her guard down once, and it had changed everything and not for the better.

But it was only a physical reaction to the calamity of the afternoon, to the sudden nearness, and the opportunity to do more. That was all.

She only hated that it was Hawk that had stirred such a response in her.

She set down her tea, knowing she couldn't drink it, and giving up pretending she would, she let her eyes drift to the other side of the room where Audrey argued with her mother over the invitations.

"We do not wish for this to be an elaborate affair," Audrey said. "We want to focus on celebrating with those who matter most to us. Friends and family members only, Mother."

Aunt Eugenia scoffed. "You really should leave this to me, Audrey. Weddings are delicate societal matters, and your guest list is a critical piece of the event. I know better—"

"No, Mother, you don't," Audrey interrupted and selected a sheet of paper from those scattered on the table in the corner before them. "This is the guest list, and that is all. We are not inviting the entirety of the *ton*."

Aunt Eugenia opened her mouth as if to object, but Audrey cut her off.

"That is it, Mother." Her tone held a note of warning.

Six months ago Caroline would not have thought Audrey had it in her to stand up to her mother, but now it seemed Aunt Eugenia rather expected it. This didn't stop her from turning her nose up at her daughter.

"If that's the way you feel, so be it. It's not as if it's my wedding. Be the fool of society if you so wish."

"I'd love to be the fool of society if it means I must not parade about in front of a bunch of silly twits who care more for the cut of their dress than they do for the bride and groom."

Aunt Eugenia's eyes widened but instead of saying anything further, she left the room.

Caroline blinked at the empty doorway through which Aunt Eugenia had disappeared.

"If this is what all of the planning is to be like, I'm afraid I shall require a great deal more stamina with which to endure it."

Audrey's smile was soft as though she had not just had an altercation with her mother. "I'm afraid that is how the whole of my life has gone. You know as much."

Caroline stood and wandered over to the table where Audrey had scattered some paper samples for the invitations.

"I'm sorry it must be that way. I would have thought with the announcement of your engagement your mother would relent."

Audrey laughed. "Hardly. It just gives her more reasons to fret. If only she knew the half of it."

Caroline stilled, her fingers extended in the direction of a particularly lovely sheet of ivory paper.

"Knew the half of what?"

Audrey slid her a glance. "Of how Dash and I came to be."

Caroline straightened and blinked. "There's rather a lot of us who know how you and Dash came to be as you put it," she said, referring to that singularly beautiful afternoon in which Audrey had stood up to her mother by proclaiming her lack of virtue. The suggestion being that Dash had taken it.

Caroline had found the entire thing both refreshing and terrifying. Audrey could not have known how her mother would react, and yet she had laid herself bare with a courage at which Caroline could only gape.

Audrey laughed and shuffled through the papers on the table. "That's hardly the half of it."

Caroline couldn't stop blinking. "What do you mean?"

Audrey glanced up again, and she must have seen something on Caroline's face because her expression sobered.

"You must realize Dash and I were carrying on quite the affair," she said, her tone low as if she remembered she was still not safely wed and thus shielded from some of the scandal her words stirred.

Caroline felt the earth shift beneath her feet again, and she pressed a hand into the cool, unforgiving surface of the table. "No, I'm afraid I hadn't realized."

Audrey straightened, concern wrinkling her brow. "Truly? I thought surely you would have caught on to us."

"Caught on to what?"

It was slipping away from her again, and she swallowed to snatch it back. Control. She had control of this situation. It wasn't as though everything were not as it seemed.

Audrey snuck a surreptitious peek at the door as if she didn't want to be caught checking their surroundings. She leaned in. "You know how I refused Dash's offer of courtship?"

Caroline nodded, and her chest tightened with...was that anticipation? How could she possibly be enjoying this recount of Audrey's secret life?

And more, how could Audrey have a secret life about which Caroline knew nothing?

How terrifying, how tumultuous, how...intriguing.

Audrey shrugged, and lowering her tone even further,

she whispered, "Well, when I refused him, we, well..." She licked her lips. "We became lovers."

Caroline nearly swallowed her tongue at the sensual word.

Lovers.

Sweet, innocent, kind Audrey had taken a...lover?

Caroline shook her head as if to rid her mind of the clamoring thoughts and spun away from the table, the invitations, and Audrey.

A lover?

Her quiet cousin had taken a lover and Caroline hadn't known?

She spun back to Audrey. "How long did you carry on your...your..."

She couldn't say the word.

Affair.

Even the very idea of it was littered with danger. Caroline's mind raced with the potential for disaster. They could have been discovered. Audrey would have been ruined. Dash would have been lauded. Aunt Eugenia would have suffered a stroke.

Caroline's head snapped up.

"You told your mother about it." She gestured around the room. "And Grandmother Regina and Aunt Verity and —" She choked on the word and stepped to the place just in front of Audrey. "You even told Ethan," Caroline hissed, referring to Audrey's most formidable brother.

Audrey smiled. "I told them all I had lost my virtue, but that seems so innocent a thing compared to the truth."

Caroline felt as though the air had been snatched from her lungs.

"What is the truth?" She found herself whispering.

Audrey looked up as though gathering her thoughts.

Finally she met Caroline's gaze. "I'm afraid Dash ruined me several times in fact."

"Audrey." Caroline's tone was scolding, even though she hadn't meant it to be, but Audrey only smiled.

"It was glorious, Caroline. I wish I could have told you about it at the time."

Glorious?

Caroline thought not.

Riddled with potential peril? Fraught with danger?

Those were both entirely more fitting.

"Well, you're getting married now, so I suppose everything turned out all right."

Audrey's brow wrinkled again. "I had no intention of marrying Dash when we became lovers."

Caroline backed up until her legs hit a chair, and she sat, no longer able to stand.

"Audrey, how could you have risked your reputation like that?"

How could she have risked her heart?

Audrey looked about her. "What reputation? I was a wallflower. No one would have noticed in the least."

"But Dash...Dash nearly destroyed you. He—"

Audrey sank on the low table before her and took Caroline's hands into her own. "Dash did not destroy me. Hurt me, yes. But no one has the power to destroy me." She shook her head. "Only I am in charge of what happens to me."

Caroline blinked. "That's not how it works."

"It is if you decide it is."

Her cousin's words washed over her, and for a moment, Caroline wondered if they were true. But then she remembered her mother when she'd discovered her husband's betrayal, and Caroline knew Audrey's idea to be a cozy fairy tale. Emotions could be traitorous.

"I'm not sure that's quite how it works."

Audrey squeezed her hands. "Caroline, do you remember my determination to be a spinster?"

Caroline nodded.

"I had no need for a husband, but Dash would not relent. So, what did I do?"

Caroline blinked. "You took him as a lover apparently."

Audrey's laugh was light and pitifully whimsical as if she were remembering that time in her life with glee. It couldn't have been all that long ago, Caroline realized, and she felt the shift of time like a tangible thing.

"Exactly. I decided. I made my life into what I wished it to be."

Caroline frowned. "But society says—"

"Hang society. When have we ever done anything the rules tell us to?"

This was rather true.

Audrey squeezed her hands again. "And don't forget what I did after I was ruined."

"Everyone who matters knows you've been ruined, Audrey. I hardly count that as a triumph."

Audrey shook her head. "You're missing the important bit. I was the one who told everyone. I decided."

She stood before Caroline could form a response, but it needn't matter anyway as Caroline was fairly certain she had lost the ability to form words at all because suddenly she was thinking about taking a lover in an entirely different light.

She still saw the pitfalls and potential danger, but she saw something else too.

She saw the opportunity to forge the life she dictated. She could have what she desired on her own terms and keep everything under her own control.

After all, if her quiet, innocent cousin could do it, Caroline could do it too.

HAWK SOUGHT out Philip at their club this time.

He'd learned his lesson about going to Mattingly House. Although days had passed since his encounter with Caroline, he still wasn't certain he had recovered.

The stark look on her face haunted him. The tears, the radiating sadness, the distress. It was all so unlike her, and it did things to him that he couldn't explain or control. Just the sight of her trembling lips was enough to spark a murderous rage in him directed at whomever had caused her such pain. It was entirely unlike him, and he wondered why his defenses were weakening now. He was so close to the end, only five weeks away, and yet he feared he wouldn't make it unscathed.

Philip sat to one side in a room that while not crowded certainly wasn't empty at this late hour of the day. Hawk took the chair next to his friend without being invited and plunged his fingers through his hair as he sat.

"Your sister is driving me mad," he said without greeting.

He had sought out Philip for the express reason of reminding himself why Caroline was not to be touched, and he wished to move straight into the topic of conversation if only to provide himself with some measure of relief.

Philip looked up from the newspaper he had been reading to eye him with a noted degree of skepticism. "Isn't she always upsetting you?"

"Upsetting, yes. Causing me to seek a stay at Bedlam? No."

Philip folded the newspaper into his lap. "It's as bad as all that then. What's happened this time?"

Hawk had no intention of telling Philip the truth, but he could skirt around it to illicit some kind of support from his old friend.

"She's going on and on about Dash's wedding," he said blandly.

Philip snorted and set the paper aside. "She does seem rather overwrought about the matter, doesn't she? I would think you would be happy not to be on the receiving end of her attentions at the moment."

Hawk motioned to a passing waiter for a drink before answering Philip. "I think that may be the issue. Her faculties are overextended, and I am left with the ineptitude in her ire."

"Like a misfired musket that a green lad attempts to reload," Philip murmured around the edge of his own glass.

"Something like that," Hawk answered, accepting a glass from the waiter.

They exchanged greetings with an old acquaintance as he walked by on the way to the door before Philip spoke again. "I wonder though how much of Caroline's irritability just now has to do with Audrey's wedding."

Hawk recalled the image of Caroline, lost and alone, at the breakfast table and took a large swallow of his drink.

"I should think it has everything to do with it. She's losing the only companion she's known in her life."

Philip wrinkled his brow. "It's not that surely. It's not as though Audrey is emigrating to America. I was rather referring to the fact that this is Caroline's third season, and she hasn't made a match while Audrey—and this is not my sentiment but what society has deemed—as a wallflower is set to marry an earl." Philip shrugged. "I'm not versed on how ladies think of marriage, but I like to think I'm clever enough to see how Caroline would be upset about such a development."

In his quest to keep a much-needed distance between he and Caroline, Hawk had failed to keep track of the number of seasons she had had. It had taken ten years into their acquaintance for him to realize how he felt about her, and another two to convince himself to leave her alone. In that time, she'd grown up, debuted, and entered into society. While he had tried to ignore the whole of it, there were some things he had been unable to.

Like how Caroline had glowed at her debut ball.

Absolutely *glowed*.

He took another large drink and tried to clear his mind, but the image of her at her debut ball was one of his favorites, and once conjured, it tended to linger. She'd worn a gown of soft, shimmering white that perched on her shoulders only to cascade down her curves like a lush, new-fallen snow.

He finished the rest of his drink and signaled to the waiter for another.

Philip raised an eyebrow. "She's truly upsetting you that much?"

Hawk ran a hand through his hair. "It's not entirely her. She's rather just the loudest of all my current annoyances."

"How are things going with your solicitor?" Philip asked.

Hawk looked at him sharply, an eyebrow raised in question.

"I saw him leaving the other day when I came to return that treatise on horseflesh you loaned me, remember?"

Hawk tried to remember what he had eaten for breakfast and failed terribly. The fact that Philip had been to see him, and he'd been distracted enough to forget the event entirely was not impossible.

"I assumed you were working on clearing up the state of affairs in which your grandfather left them," Philip added.

Hawk nodded as he accepted the fresh drink from the waiter, happy to be discussing something other than Caroline.

"Yes, I finally got the deeds straightened out for that parcel Grandfather purchased on the south end of the property in Hampshire. What a mess that was. Grandfather apparently agreed to an easement for the neighboring estate to move their sheep. The bloke took it as an invitation to allow his sheep to graze on Stonegate land." He shook his head. "I've unfortunately been forced to erect a new fence now that the issue of the easement has been clarified."

"I cannot fathom how your grandfather could have allowed things to become so neglected."

Hawk knew precisely how such things occurred. His grandfather was forever traveling, leaving his wife and grandson to wander about the estate alone. When Hawk had first left for school, he'd been worried his grandmother would die of loneliness, and at his first opportunity, he'd returned home to check on her. She'd never spoken of it, of course. She pretended he had forgotten something and showered him with attention until bundling him back off in the carriage bound for school.

It went on like that for the first year he was away, and then Grandfather had died somewhere in the Middle East. It still wasn't clear where it had happened, and as a child, Hawk couldn't understand why his grandfather had allowed it to happen. As an adult, Hawk knew too well.

The reason that drove his grandfather away was the same one that had Hawk tidying his affairs so Grandmother would not be left in such a precarious state again. While Hawk had lost his father, Grandfather had lost his son.

"He was more interested in his travels than in anything that was left for him here in England," Hawk decided to say.

He felt Philip's gaze on him but couldn't gather the courage to look his friend in the eye. Hawk's father might have died twenty-seven years previously, but to Hawk, he seemed to lose him every day.

Philip must have sensed the dangerous edge they stood on and changed the subject.

"My mother is hosting a ball for Audrey and Dash. You'll come, of course."

Hawk looked up at this. "Shouldn't Lady Dartford be throwing a ball for her own daughter?"

Philip shook his head. "Audrey forbids it." He pulsed his eyebrows with obvious glee. "Apparently Audrey is forbidding her mother to do many things in regard to the wedding. Caroline has been rather busy with the planning of the affair."

"Surely Lady Dartford should be happy for Audrey."

"Happy, yes," Philip said before taking another drink. "But you know she and Audrey had differing views on what the event should be."

Hawk had met Lady Dartford on several occasions and could only imagine what societal heights the woman would attempt to obtain at the expense of her daughter.

"I've heard it's supposed to be the happiest day of a young woman's life," Hawk said.

He had meant the remark flippantly, and he was surprised to see a cloud pass over Philip's face. Hawk stilled, watching his friend slowly gather himself.

"Have you...have you heard from her?" Hawk ventured.

Philip slowly slid his gaze to him, but his eyes were

rather unfocused as if seeing a different time and place. Hawk waited several beats, and Philip finally shook his head.

"Have you ever thought about inquiring after her?"

Philip held his glass in both of his hands, rolling the fine cut crystal against his open palms. Hawk watched the hypnotic gesture remotely, more aware of the pounding of his heart as he considered his friend.

"I really have no reason to contact her, do I? It's not as though..." He let the sentence drift, but Hawk saw him swallow.

Philip didn't need to finish the sentence because Hawk was one of the few people who knew the truth. Philip was not the father of Lady Winnaretta's baby. He had merely been the one who had offered to save her.

"Really? Is that what you think? I would imagine the two of you would have quite a bit to say to each other. After all that happened."

Philip's look was swift and stark. "I disagree," he said, his voice almost guttural. "I cannot for a moment understand what she must have endured, Hawk. Can you? She was... young." He said the final word loudly as if it were the only one that seemed to come out, but it wasn't the one he would have chosen. His eyes moved back and forth as if trying to find something else to say. He seemed to give up and set his glass on the table between them, dropping his head in his hands. "It's been five years, Hawk," he muttered from behind his fingers.

Hawk reached over and squeezed his friend's shoulder. "Then don't you think it's time to say something?"

Philip dropped his hands and gave Hawk a bleak look. "If I haven't said anything in five years, why should I start now?"

"Because perhaps in five years she's had time to heal and can accept your olive branch with an open mind?"

Philip appeared to consider this before shifting his gaze away. It was several moments before he said, "Winnie never wanted anything to do with me, you know."

Hawk winced. "She was grieving, Philip. And then..." But he couldn't finish the sentence because it was just too horrible to remember.

Philip slid him a dark glance that said everything Hawk was feeling.

Hawk swallowed and changed tact. "You'll never know what she truly felt unless you speak with her. I had heard somewhere that she stays in town at her family's home."

Hawk didn't miss the flinch Philip tried to hide. They both knew Lady Winnaretta had her reasons to eschew the countryside. Hawk couldn't blame her. There were likely too many memories at her family's country home.

Philip pushed abruptly to his feet. "I won't pretend to consider the matter, Hawk. You know I've never wished to make Winnie confront something she did not wish to."

Hawk stood as well. "But isn't that the point? You don't know if she wishes to speak with you or not."

Something traveled over Philip's face then, and Hawk wondered how much his friend had told him about the day when his engagement fell apart. For that was what had happened. Plans had been made. Expectations were set.

And then Winnie had lost the baby.

Hawk had watched his friend recede, and it had stunned Hawk. He hadn't realized how much Philip had come to think of the baby as his own. Not until it was already over. And then there was Winnie.

It was one of the few regrets he had in his life. That he

wasn't there for Philip when the man needed him. Hawk had still been on the continent then.

He wouldn't let him down again. At least, not for as long as he could.

So, when Philip clapped him on the back and told him he'd see him at the engagement ball, Hawk could not refuse the invitation.

4

———

Caroline watched Audrey dance with Dash.

Was it her imagination or did the orchestra play the first notes of the waltz with an extra delicacy? Did the music seem to weave through the air tangling with the glowing notes of the chandeliers? Was the warm summer night air more fragrant with the heady mixture of summer blooms?

Or was Caroline pining for Hawk?

She threw back the rest of her champagne in a single swallow.

This was not supposed to happen. In the ordered and neat world she had created for herself, emotions were to be left to the wayside. She should have been free to be bored by the evening's events and meander about in the hopes of stumbling upon some mildly interesting gossip.

Instead she stood on the periphery of the ballroom.

At least she had Grandmother Regina with her. She turned and considered the woman now, sitting primly in her seat, her shiny white hair bobbing to the music. Caroline had promised Aunt Verity she would watch Grandmother so Aunt Verity could enjoy a bit of the night's festivities, but Aunt Verity had returned far sooner than Caroline expected, looking dull and tired still but with a glass of lemonade now.

She felt another sigh coming and instead of indulging in her woe, she turned back to Audrey to find her smiling, radiantly, exorbitantly. With a sharp twist of her stomach, Caroline wished she were in her cousin's place.

The thought had her straightening. That wasn't the truth at all. She didn't wish to marry Hawk. She just wished to...

Well, perform *other* activities with him.

She could feel the heat her thoughts had sent charging up her neck. The room swayed around her or perhaps she swayed. Aunt Verity was suddenly by her side, plucking the empty champagne glass from her fingers.

"Caroline, are you ill? You look quite flustered."

Grandmother Regina patted Caroline's hand. "Dear, dear, you should go outside for a spot of air. You look as though you've seen a ghost."

Caroline thought she nodded in agreement, but her thoughts were tumbling one atop the other, and she couldn't be sure of anything.

The terrace provided little relief as the night was warm, nearly sultry, and she made her way to the shadows at the far end.

She could have mapped the entire garden of Mattingly House in the dark if she wished, and she had no trouble at all slipping from the stone terrace into the gardens proper. She left the fieldstone path, and as soon as her slippers touched grass, she shucked them, carrying them in the fingers of one hand. Her stockings would be ruined, but she didn't care. She only wished for the comforting darkness of the familiar gardens.

She turned down one path and then another until she was deep within the circle of hedges that bordered the center of the garden, but instead of moving deeper, she turned east. Once, very long ago, her mother had installed rose bowers that ran along the path to the east gardens, and in the moonlight, Caroline could make out the heavy blossoms that formed the floral tunnel.

She didn't stop until she broke free from the path, and moonlight spilled around her. She wasn't sure when she had begun to think of the folly as her secret place, but it had always been that way, and now she slipped over the familiar flagstones until she reached the steps.

It was chinoiserie in design, and even in the moonlight its red lacquer finish glowed. The roof spread up into a golden finial, and its copper panels had turned green with age. She left the door ajar, allowing the night air to seep in. Some time ago she had brought cushions to the folly and had ordered a rug to be laid out, and she was grateful now as she sank into those cushions.

She had nearly reclined entirely when something sharp stabbed her side. She sat up and held aloft her dance card, hanging accusingly from her wrist. She tossed it aside and finally, blissfully leaned back, and there it was.

The stars.

Painted across the sky as if only for her. The generous window panels of the folly allowed her to see clear up to the dotted expanse, and she studied it now, feeling the tension ease from her shoulders.

Until she heard a sound at the door.

She sat up so quickly the room spun, and her hair pins

caught against the cushions, tugging some of her hair loose to fall against her shoulders.

"Hawk."

He was trying to escape unnoticed. How odd.

How odd that he had followed her.

He turned back slowly, his hand still on the doorframe.

He didn't look at her as he said, "I was simply ensuring your safety."

She looked about her. "From whom?"

The only person she was in any danger from had followed her into the folly. As he was unaware of his suddenly changed position, she didn't think him all that much of a threat.

He didn't come any closer. He folded his arms over his chest and leaned against the doorframe. He was silhouetted in moonlight, and she couldn't help but notice how his hair darkened to a decadent brown in the dim light.

"Yourself," he said.

If only he knew...

She sat up straighter, tucking her legs beneath her skirts, suddenly aware of her lack of shoes.

"I would think you would prefer to be in the ballroom chasing after some light skirt."

This was entirely unlike him, but she was feeling rather defensive.

He closed his eyes slowly, and only after a couple of beats did he open them again.

"I thought it would be more fun to irritate you for a space, pet." His teeth shone white through the darkness when he smiled with mocking pleasure.

She worried why she didn't find the annoying endearment...well, annoying.

"Bored with the season already? I do hope I can provide some entertainment. I haven't seen you with Philip very often of late. Am I to understand I have won our battle?" She gestured between them as if with a flick of her hand she could encompass the whole of their complicated relationship.

Now he did straighten away from the door, taking two steps toward her.

"Is that what this is? A battle? I thought you were just bored and annoying."

"I am both of those things, but that's hardly the point here."

She had forgotten the point actually. When he moved so slowly through the shadows, his austere evening attire blending with the night…she forgot nearly everything.

She rolled and pushed to her feet, brushing her hands against her skirts in a weak attempt at propriety.

"Do you remember when we were children, and you and Philip chased me out here? I can't remember what it was you chased me with, but I recall it to be terribly frightening."

The sound of his soft laugh was startling, and she turned to study him. He rubbed at the back of his neck before saying, "Mud. We had made a mess of one of the garden beds and threatened to fling mud at you." He laughed again. "I had forgotten about that."

She tilted her head, allowing her gaze to linger on him.

"What is it?" he asked after some moments.

"Your laugh sounds so unused. Is everything all right?" She shouldn't have asked the question. She wasn't supposed to care a fig about him, but he appeared small and lost just then. Maybe it was a trick of the moon, the way it slanted through the glass panels. Maybe it was her own heightened emotions. Maybe it was nothing at all.

Except he didn't answer her right away. He only watched her as she watched him. The night air was thick around them, and she longed to lift the curtain of her hair from her neck, but she couldn't move.

Something was happening between them.

It was as though their entire relationship up until this point was rearranging itself, shifting to form a new state of being. It was almost as if she could reach out and grasp it and force everything back to the way it had been, but she couldn't do it. She was helpless and hopeful at the same time.

He drew a breath, and she thought he would say something, but he remained silent, his eyes moving over her as if he'd changed his mind. Once more, she thought he looked sad, but Hawkins Savage had nothing over which to be sad.

Unless he was sad because he wanted her, and he thought...what was the word she had used? Battle. He thought they were at war with one another.

She didn't want to be at war with him.

She took a step toward him. Stopped. Waited. Tried to sort through her emotions.

She knew what she should do. She should leave. March past him and out into the night to find Philip. She should keep Hawk far away from her and her family.

But what she wanted to do was entirely different.

Dimly she became aware of the sound of music floating on the night air, and she pictured her cousin, her best friend in all the world, dancing, resplendent in the arms of the man she loved.

She stepped forward at the same time Hawk did, and they were in each other's arms.

His mouth came down on hers in a hot, searing kiss, and

she arched into him, her fingers finding the crest of his shoulders so she could pull herself closer to him.

Their embrace at the house party seemed a lifetime ago, and now she learned his body anew. The hard planes of his chest and stomach. The broad curve of his shoulders. Had the stubble of his beard been this rough before? Had it stroked her skin in teasing caresses the way it did now?

She groaned and he pulled her beneath him, holding her with one arm as he lowered them to the rug. She fell back against the cushions as he came atop her, his lips never leaving hers.

Heat surged through her body, pooling low in her belly. She freed a leg from her cloying skirts to wrap around his, wanting to feel more of him.

"Caroline." He'd left her mouth to press his lips against her jaw, her cheeks, her temple. "Caroline, what are we doing?"

She silenced him with a kiss, not wanting to talk, not wanting to reason. She only wanted to feel.

She wanted to feel...better. That was what he had done at the house party. That was what he had made her feel. He had taken away the tension that haunted her, the fear of things slipping from her control.

For just a moment, she wanted this. She wanted him. She wanted to feel...alive.

Later she would think about the rest of it. Later she would try to reason with herself. Try to convince herself this wasn't real. That nothing good could come from it.

That if she gave him her heart, he would crush it.

She winced at the thought, and Hawk started to pull away.

She cupped his face in her hands, opening her eyes to catch his.

"Hawk." Her voice was low and thick, and she swallowed, tried again. "Hawk. Please."

Everything inside of her tightened all at once. She knew what she wanted to say. She knew what she wanted to ask of him.

But even the thought of saying the words had her freezing in fear.

For if she spoke them, she was giving some of her power away.

But then the moonlight shifted, falling across his face, and she saw the stark look in his eyes again.

She shifted her hand, smoothing the wrinkle of his brow.

"Hawk, I want you to make love to me. Tonight. Just tonight, Hawk. One night is all I want."

The words hung in the air between them, but he didn't speak. He didn't move. The fear rose up in her, and when she thought it would drown her, he spoke.

"All right," he said and kissed her.

~

ALL RIGHT?

That was what he had said?

He had had his fair share of affairs. Nothing extravagant or bordering on debauchery. But enough he felt confident he could have come up with something better than all right, but here he was.

Kissing Caroline.

Again.

Only this was so much worse because she was under him, and they were alone.

Again.

What was he doing? He shouldn't be here. He shouldn't have followed her.

No, that wasn't right. He shouldn't have sought her out in the ballroom. When he'd come across Lady Verity and Grandmother Regina, he had been surprised to find Caroline was not with them. Audrey was practically effervescent as she filtered through the room on Dash's arm, and Hawk worried how it might affect Caroline.

Only when he'd gone to find her, she wasn't where he thought she would be.

Grandmother Regina had said she'd gone out for some air, and Lady Verity had pointed him in the direction of the terrace.

It might have been her own home, but he wasn't going to allow her to wander the gardens in the dark with so many guests scampering about. He'd caught sight of her almost immediately, an ethereal lightness against the dark backdrop of the gardens.

He had meant to call out to her, but then she'd removed her slippers. Right there on the grass, one by one, she'd popped them from her feet. He had been transfixed by the sight of it, his words catching in his throat.

And then another thought had hit him.

What if she were going to meet someone?

Philip's words from the previous day at the club rang in his ears, and he worried Caroline might take desperate measures to secure a match. It didn't seem possible. Nothing about Caroline spoke of desperation, but then he couldn't forget how she had looked that morning in the breakfast room.

Perhaps she *could* be so daring.

The idea had had his stomach clenching painfully, and he hadn't given it another thought. He'd just gone after her.

She'd never hesitated in her trek through the shadowy gardens, and he knew instantly where she must be going.

Hawk had spent some holidays at Mattingly House, especially when his grandmother married again after his grandfather's death. He and Philip had used the gardens for their games, and Hawk was fairly sure he could find his way about the place blindfolded.

Which was good because when Caroline ducked out of sight, he needn't rush. He knew exactly where she was going.

He had also known the kind of privacy her destination afforded, and a hot spike of jealousy tore through him.

Jealousy and something deeper, darker, and more ferocious. It terrified him at the same time it felt expected.

So, when he discovered her, reclined in a lush pile of cushions, her stockinged toes curling into a thick rug, her eyes focused longingly at the night sky, something in him had been rendered useless.

He had tried to retreat. That would be his defense until his dying day. But the sight of her, so vulnerable, so exposed, so...not angry at him for something she had imagined, was too much. He'd slipped on the first stair in his retreat and thus had made a sound, giving away his presence.

He had expected her to be angry that he followed her and more that he had interrupted her quiet interlude. But he hadn't expected her to be...nostalgic.

He hadn't thought she had any good memories of him. Not that the time he had threatened to fling mud at her was a good memory, but she had seemed warmed by it.

But even then, when her face was light with memory, there was a sadness that had lurked about her eyes.

It was this sadness that had gotten him in the end.

When she had kissed him—or had he kissed her?—all

of his defenses had been obliterated. It was as though all of his resolve, all of his determination, had vanished at the bleakness in her eyes.

And now he was all but mauling her, here in this place where they'd once tramped with mud in their childish games.

"Hawk," she groaned his name against his lips, and it was as though he'd plunged into an icy river.

He jerked his head back, breaking the kiss.

"We can't do this. Caroline, we can't." But he didn't let go of her. He didn't attempt to stand and flee.

He stayed where he was, nestled between her legs and ensconced in that ridiculous pile of cushions.

"Yes, but we should do it," she countered, reaching up to draw him back to her.

He stilled her with a hand on her wrist. "What do you mean?"

Her eyes searched his face. "Can't you see? It's just one night. One night means very little in the whole of one's life. If just for tonight—"

He leaned back on his knees, taking her captured hand in both of his as he tried to cool his desire.

"It's not one night, Caroline. It would ruin you and any chance for your future."

She scoffed and sat up, using their combined hands to tug him against her. "Only if someone finds out."

"Someone always finds out." He could not be having this conversation right now. Not with anyone, but especially not with Caroline.

"No, they won't. Hawk." She sat up farther, adjusting herself around his bent legs, and he swallowed, willing his composure to remain intact. "Do you know Dash and Audrey were—are, I suppose—having an affair?"

He raised an eyebrow. "I had a feeling as much."

Caroline's lips parted without sound emerging for several seconds. "You did? But how?"

He shook his head and leaned back until he was sitting on the rug, his passion slowly ebbing but his mind still foggy. He scrubbed his hands over his face.

"It was obvious," he said but the astonished look on her face didn't disappear. "The way they look at each other when they think no one sees them? The way Dash seemed to always appear at her elbow? The way he followed her at the house party?" Still the astonished look remained. "Caroline, please tell me you noticed."

Something swept over her face then, clouding it, and he felt a sharp stab of fear as though he had touched one of her old wounds he didn't know existed.

"No, I didn't notice," she said more quietly and tugged at her legs for him to shift off her skirts. Once freed, she tucked her legs up against her chest and wrapped her arms around them.

Cold descended on him. He had trodden on a sore subject for her, and yet he didn't know what it could be. Was it still about losing her companion to marriage? That didn't seem likely. She had been sad and lost when he'd found her at the breakfast table, but the way she held herself so carefully now, so guarded, this was something else, something deeper, darker, and more scarring.

What had he prodded and how deep did the wound run?

He leaned forward, elbows on his knees. "Haven't you ever been in love, pet?"

He used her nickname purposefully, hoping to draw her out of this shell she had erected. How could a woman be so passionate and vulnerable in his arms only to turn to stone minutes later?

Her eyes flashed to his. "No, I have not, and I'm grateful to say so."

Something thudded in his stomach. "I beg your pardon."

She lifted her chin. "Love is a silly notion that makes one do silly things."

"You can't really believe that."

"I do, in fact." She rocked forward as if to emphasize her point. "I've witnessed it."

He had been about to retort, but this changed his mind. She'd witnessed it? He sifted through his memories, his mind stumbling across a boulder.

He frowned. "This is about Philip, isn't it?"

There. There was a moment's hesitation. Her eyes moving ever so slightly to the left before she said, "Yes. Yes, that's it." Her words stumbled, tripping from her lips as she struggled to meet his eyes.

What a little liar.

So, what was it then? What had her believing something so sinister about love? His chest tightened, and he wanted to rub a hand against the sudden pain there. He wished he were so afraid to love.

"So, because of Philip's wilder days you have foresworn love. What about marriage?"

She wrinkled her nose. "Never. I would never attach myself to another."

He wasn't sure why he hadn't considered this. Somehow he had thought along the same lines as Philip. That Caroline would wish to wed and see Audrey's impending marriage as further pressure to find her own match.

But that didn't appear to be it at all.

"So, you're not upset that Audrey is marrying before you. You're upset that she's marrying at all."

Caroline opened her mouth but seemed to think better of it. She looked up as if gathering her thoughts. "No. No, that's not it. I think Audrey will truly enjoy marriage." She lowered her gaze to his. "I hope she and Dash are very happy together."

He raised an eyebrow. "But you won't fall in love."

"Never."

Again, such a strong word spoken so quickly. A chill crept through him.

"Then what is this about? Here. Tonight." He gestured between them.

She lowered her knees, her hands in her lap. "It was rather a practical thought. There's obviously something going on between us that neither of us is finding particularly enjoyable."

He disagreed with that but allowed her to continue.

"I thought if we were to, as they say, scratch the itch, we could get it out of our minds."

He raised both eyebrows now. "One night? You think one night would be enough to quell this?"

She canted her head. "Of course. Why wouldn't it?"

He shook his head but couldn't bring himself to speak.

She straightened, pressing her hands into her lap. "Do you have something you'd like to say about it?"

He caught her gaze, keeping his tone cool. "I think you're incredibly naive." He got to his feet. "But then I'm not surprised given how quickly you are to blame me for the problems of others."

She surged more than stood, her skirts billowing around her. "Naive? I am naive? You lured Philip into Lady

Winnaretta's clutches and expected nothing to happen. How am I the naive one?"

"I didn't—" He bit the inside of his cheek and turned away from her, burying his face in his hands before turning back. "I'm leaving. The gentlemanly thing for me to do is escort you back to the house."

She crossed her arms over her chest. "And when have you ever been a gentleman?"

He headed for the door without looking at her again until she spoke.

"Hawk."

He closed his eyes, his hand hanging in the air, almost to the door. Why must she use his given name?

He turned back.

"If you believe in love so much, why are you not wed?"

The answer was right there. It sprang to his lips on a spark of vibrating anger. He could tell her. He could tell her everything right now. Lady Winnaretta's secret, Philip's hurt, and his own imminent demise. He could spill it all and end this. He could *end it* right now.

The moon slanted through the windows and illuminated her in all her mussed glory. Her golden hair like a halo about her head, her wrinkled skirts hanging loosely about her stockinged legs. Her stockinged feet still pressing into the carpet.

God, would he always be felled by her toes?

He met her gaze. "The only person I would ever wish to marry is you, but you've never seemed inclined to accept my suit."

He left without another word but not before he heard her startled gasp.

5

She wasn't sure how long she stood there, but it was long enough to fuel the anger that bubbled inside of her.

Why did he always do this to her?

How could he stir such anger and confusion at the same time he planted hope and curiosity?

Why was nothing about Hawkins Savage simple?

When her feet grew cold against the carpet, she rooted around for her slippers, shoving her hair from her face. She couldn't possibly return to the ball like this. She would need to sneak around the back and hope the library doors had been left unlocked. She would make her way up to her rooms, and should her absence be noted, she would lie and say she'd gone to bed with a headache.

She did, in fact, have a headache, but that was the least of her concerns.

After several minutes, she gave up the search for her second slipper and left the folly. She'd come back in the daylight and see if she could find where it had ended up. With one hand on her slipper, she used the other to tame her hair into some kind of order, tucking it behind her ears. Should she run into anyone else scampering through the gardens, she would look at least mildly presentable.

As long as she kept conversation to a minimum, she just might make it.

He wished to marry only her?

Had he truly said as much?

What a wastrel.

What a scoundrel.

What a—

She stopped, dew soaking through her stockings as her body released a sigh that traveled from the top of her head directly down to her toes.

What an infuriating man.

One moment she was convinced of his devious and apathetic ways when it came to Philip, and the next she feared she was falling in love with him.

If only the divine universe would give her an answer and for once and for all she could understand the true Hawk, she could set aside her torment and move on with her life.

As a spinster.

She halted once more, her slipper falling forgotten against her thigh.

She was going to be a spinster.

While she had known for so long that she would never marry, it had never occurred to her in such terms.

Spinster.

Caroline Hodge, the daughter of the Marquess of Mattingly, the belle of every ball, the most sought-after debutante in her season.

She blinked into the darkness, the summer air cloying as it pressed against her neck.

Well, so be it. She would never give herself to a man. She would never relinquish power over her person.

Then why did her future suddenly feel so lonely?

She forged on, her feet sinking into the damp grass as the lights of the house grew brighter, the sounds of merriment and music growing more distinct.

Unless she married Hawk.

She nearly fell into the rose bower as she passed beneath it.

She wasn't marrying Hawk. Firstly, he hadn't asked. Secondly, it was *Hawk*.

But God, she longed to kiss him again. Her body ached with what might have been, and her emotions were left in a confused state of dissatisfaction.

That was it. It was purely physical. If only she'd had the opportunity to quell her curiosity, she wouldn't feel so unsettled. That was all.

Her headache was worse, pounding against her temples, but she ignored it and pressed farther toward the house. She skirted the terrace off the ballroom, traveling through the shadows in the direction of the library.

She rounded the last hedge, her hand already extending to open the library door when it collided with a person.

"Oh!" The exclamation flew from her lips before she could stop it, her slipper falling from her fingers in surprise.

She peered into the shadows. It was so much darker here, away from the bustle of the ball, and it was that much more difficult to make out the person she had inadvertently assaulted. "Miss Holloway?"

If the light had been better, Caroline would have sworn Miss Holloway blushed.

"Pippa, please, Lady Caroline. I'm so sorry to have disturbed."

Caroline crossed her arms over her chest. "Disturbed me? I think that's rather the other way around. I nearly trod directly over you."

Again Caroline gathered a sense of sheepishness from the paid companion.

As it was there was the sound of deprecation in the woman's voice when she answered, "Oh no, it's entirely my fault. I shouldn't be lurking in shadows. Especially at a ball."

While Caroline could understand what Pippa implied, her thoughts were stubbornly focused on the practical. "Because you should be seeing to Lady Spader?"

Pippa hesitated. "Yes, that's it. It's only...well, her snores do grow tiresome."

Caroline caught the hint of a smile on the woman's face and smiled in understanding.

"She's fallen asleep again then?"

Lady Spader was prone to falling asleep at social gatherings, and Caroline did not understand why the woman had a companion at all. It wasn't as though she were awake to enjoy the woman's company.

"I'm afraid she has," Pippa replied quietly.

Caroline nodded and bent to find her slipper in the grass. "I do hope I can trust you to not tell anyone you found me out here in the dark."

Pippa's smile was brighter now when Caroline straightened. "Only if you promise not to tell on me."

Caroline laughed. "I shouldn't think of it. A woman has a right to some solitude when she should find it."

"Thank you, Lady Caroline."

Caroline shook her head. "Please call me Caroline." She reached out and squeezed the paid companion's arm. She was about to bid the woman good evening when something stopped her.

Caroline stepped back and assessed the woman, a suspicion crawling up her neck.

"Pippa," Caroline began, her thoughts still rather jumbled even as she spoke. "You were familiar with the Earl of Amberley's reputation, were you not?"

Once, what seemed a lifetime ago, Pippa had provided valuable information regarding Dash's reputation. It suddenly occurred to Caroline that a woman in Pippa's position may know a great deal more.

"Yes, I did. It's hard not to know of the man's reputation when I've been privy to hearing about it from all manner of ladies visiting Lady Spader."

Caroline nodded. "Do you happen to know anything about the Earl of Stonegate?"

Why was she doing this?

Why was she asking about Hawk? Why did she care? Part of her woke in alarm at what she might discover. Would it help resolve her turbulent emotions or would it only serve to exacerbate them?

"Lord Stonegate? I should say I know him quite well."

Caroline wasn't sure how it happened, but her entire body stilled. She worried even her heart had stopped beating, and her lungs had ceased to gather air.

"Lord Stonegate? You...know him?"

Pippa nodded furiously, her eyes wide in the darkness. "Lord Stonegate is a parishioner in my father's parish in Surrey."

Surrey. Stonegate Manor was in Surrey.

"Is that so?" It was a silly question to ask, but suddenly Caroline wished to not appear eager.

Pippa nodded again. "Lord Stonegate attends services with his grandmother when he is in residence at the manor. He never misses a Sunday."

Caroline blinked as though this would help to settle the rampage of questions that surged through her at the idea of Hawk escorting his grandmother to Sunday services. The same Hawk who had single-handedly orchestrated her brother's near ruin.

Caroline swallowed. Hawk may behave the gentleman where his grandmother was concerned, but that meant nothing about the rest of him.

"I see," Caroline said now. "That's rather kind of him."

Pippa nodded with greater certainty. "Lord Stonegate is a very kind gentleman. I was rather surprised to find he has a radically different reputation here in London. At least from what I've been able to gather of it since I've arrived here."

Caroline's heart began beating again with a walloping thud. "A different reputation?"

It was difficult to ascertain the details of Pippa's expression in the darkness, but it appeared her brow wrinkled in concern. "Well, you see Lord Stonegate is a great patron of the poor in my father's parish. Should a man be seeking coin, Lord Stonegate always finds him a proper job on his estate. He's never one to give a handout, but rather he strives to honor a man's pride and give him the means of improving himself." Pippa shook her head. "I must admit when I first arrived I didn't think it was the same Lord Stonegate. He's rather jolly, and he does seem to enjoy teasing you, Lady Caroline. Er, Caroline." She smiled unsteadily.

Teasing.

If only it were so innocent.

The image Pippa painted of Hawk did not fit with the picture Caroline had constructed of him. It was easier to think of Hawk as the reckless, cavalier entitled dandy, but she was coming to understand that her perception of him may be tainted from their shared history.

But she couldn't let it go. She couldn't release that tarnished idea of Hawk because if she did...

Then she had no excuse for pushing him away.

If he were the revered gentleman Pippa claimed him to be, if he was the doting grandson, if he was the responsible landowner, if he was....

Her brother's best friend.

She hardened her jaw. "How long have you known Lord Stonegate then?"

Pippa shrugged. "I can't say as I know. Likely since we were children he was attending services, but I imagine he was at school a great deal. There were long absences in our childhood, and I was always helping my father. I couldn't say as I always knew who attended services. It wasn't until later that—" Oddly Pippa's voice strangled off, and she paused to swallow harshly. "I'm sorry. I think I might be in need of refreshment."

The woman moved to pick up her skirts as though she may return to the ballroom, but Caroline held out a hand, catching the woman's arm.

"Pippa, if I may, I'd like to ask you one more question." The alarm grew greater inside her chest, burning with a hotness that seemed far too real, but suddenly the question was there, lingering on her lips, and she feared Pippa would have an answer. "As you are privy to a great number of social gatherings, I was wondering if you have reason to be acquainted with Lady Winnaretta Lowe."

The question was out, and with it, Caroline's heart hammered in her chest.

But Pippa's eyes narrowed as if in contemplation. "Lady

Winnaretta Lowe?" She shook her head. "I can't say as I know of the lady."

Caroline deflated, her heart falling into a sluggish beat. What had she expected? Lady Winnaretta had not been seen in society since her broken engagement. Why should Pippa have become acquainted with her?

Caroline squeezed the woman's arm. "Thank you. You've indulged me quite enough, and I'm sorry to have kept you."

Pippa laughed, the sound soft but slightly unsure as if the woman weren't used to laughing. "I can assure you it was no trouble at all. I have appreciated the respite." Her smile was steadier now, her white teeth showing in the dark.

Caroline nodded. "If you ever have an afternoon, I'd love to have you for tea."

Pippa's eyes flared wide as if startled, but Caroline was by far more startled. The invitation had suddenly sprung to her lips of its own accord, and she wondered if she were scrambling to find a replacement for Audrey. Her stomach twisted, and the headache that pounded at her temples raged anew.

Everything was changing. Absolutely everything, and she wasn't sure if she could survive it.

But then Pippa smiled, and Caroline realized what a kind, gracious woman the paid companion was.

"I should love that," she said.

They bid each other good night and parted in the darkness. Caroline slipped into the library and up the servants' stairs to her rooms. It was only when she closed the door behind her that she allowed herself the luxury of sinking to the floor and burying her face in her upturned knees.

∾

"Out for a stroll in the gardens?"

Hawk stopped so abruptly he nearly overturned a potted fern flanking the door to the gaming rooms.

Philip stood at the edge of the gaming tables, serenely sipping some champagne and smiling mischievously.

"Were you watching me?" Hawk narrowed his gaze.

Philip laughed. "No. Grandmother Regina said you'd gone to ensure Caroline was all right. I understand she's upset about Audrey's marriage." His expression folded with concern. "I hadn't realized how much this would affect her."

Happy to have the focus on the conversation moved away from him, Hawk said, "Audrey is her best friend. I imagine with the limited freedom ladies have, female friendship is valued highly."

Philip took another swallow of champagne, but Hawk didn't miss the way he flinched. "I suppose you're right."

He nodded at a passing acquaintance before taking Hawk's arm and steering him out of the gaming room and into the buffet room. At this hour, the room was largely deserted, and the sudden quiet was alarming.

He was still attempting to recover himself from the encounter in the garden, and the ringing the silence left in his ears was startling. He ran a hand through his hair and snatched a glass from a passing footman's tray.

Running into Philip had not been his plan when he'd come back through the ballroom. He had thought to get a drink and lose a large sum of monies at the card table if only to distract himself.

He knew it was reckless and unwise, but just then, the thought of anything else that might take away the sting of his latest encounter with Caroline was highly appealing no matter its sinful qualities.

"I trust you found Caroline to be in good company."

Philip drew them away from the tables of food to a corner littered with chairs. He took one and leaned back, resting an arm over his crossed knee.

Hawk took the adjacent seat. "Yes, she was quite fine. She just wished for some air." His words sounded stilted to his own ears, and he hoped Philip didn't notice.

"I would worry about some rake trying to take advantage of her, but then I remember it's Caroline." He smiled but it was more a show of his teeth. "And I worry more for the rake who would attempt it than I do my sister." He laughed, but the sound was hollow.

Hawk watched him closely, and for the first time, he noticed Philip's look of...what? Regret? Hurt? Despair? It seemed his sister's lack of a match was affecting him more than he let on, and what he had learned only minutes before burned hotter in his chest.

Hawk swallowed some champagne. "No, it was nothing like that. I think it's just a lot of change for her to grapple at once." He eyed Philip. "You know how she is with sudden changes in her direct vicinity."

Philip outwardly cringed now. "It's been five years, and it's not as if I were the injured party in it. You would think she would forget about it by now."

Hawk shook his head. "It seems your near ruin may have struck an old wound."

He couldn't help but remember the look that had passed over Caroline's face when he mentioned marriage. There was something that haunted her, and he was beginning to wonder if it had to do with something other than Philip's broken engagement.

"An old wound? Caroline?" Philip's voice rose in question. "What has Caroline to be wounded about?"

It was as though fate were listening, and at that moment,

Lady Mattingly floated into the room, her gown billowing out behind her like she would have forgotten it had she not been wearing it. Her gaze was unfocused, and her footsteps soft and hesitant as if she weren't certain on a destination.

Philip dropped his foot to the ground, pitching forward in his seat as if preparing to stand. He watched his mother quietly, but Hawk could see the tension in his friend's shoulders, the set of his jaw.

"Philip, has your mother always been like this?" Hawk asked the question softly, both because he didn't wish for someone to hear him and because it was a delicate question.

Philip's gaze narrowed as if he were considering his answer. "I can remember a time when she was quite fun actually." He turned, facing Hawk. "But that was a very long time ago now."

Hawk licked his lips, feeling trepidation like a wave about to smother him. "What happened?"

Philip's shrug was shallow as if he didn't enjoy his answer. "I don't know. Once when I came home on school holiday everything had changed. The house was quieter, Caroline was angrier, and Mother..." His voice trailed off as he gestured to her.

Lady Mattingly had moved across the room to the buffet tables, but she didn't select any food. She just regarded the tables, her eyes roving over the surface unseeing.

"Did Caroline ever say what happened?"

Philip shook his head. "I asked once, but you know Caroline."

"She became defensive." Hawk didn't need to make it a question.

"Something like that," Philip muttered as his mother moved again, this time to the opposite end of the room from them.

There was nothing down there for guests, and servants passed through a set of doors in the rear corner from time to time.

Briefly Philip glanced in his direction. "I suppose after that my father became scarce around the house. He was gone more frequently, and I think at the time I was more preoccupied with my own happenings than to ask where he might be going."

Philip held his gaze for several seconds, and Hawk could fill in the rest. Had Lord Mattingly taken a lover? Had this upset his wife? What did Caroline know of it?

Instead of answers, he had more questions, but just then, Lady Mattingly attempted to follow a servant precariously balancing a tray of empty champagne glasses below stairs.

Philip got to his feet, and Hawk followed him, a hand on his friend's arm.

"Allow me." Hawk stepped forward, eating up the carpet with his long strides as he made his way to the other end of the room. "Lady Mattingly!" he called, curving his voice with a vibrant note.

She hardly started even though several heads in the room turned toward him.

"Lady Mattingly, I thought you had saved me a dance." He plastered on his brightest smile when she turned, and it was as though whatever spell had been cast over her had suddenly vanished, and her face relaxed into some semblance of cognition.

"Hawk, dear. Whatever are you talking about? You know I don't dance." Her eyes moved behind him. "Did my son put you up to some sort of jest?"

He had reached her and bowed extravagantly. "Nothing

of the sort, Lady Mattingly. It is only that I wish to dance with the most beautiful woman at the ball."

Lady Mattingly's laugh was hollow. "Now I know you're jesting." She turned fully and began to walk back to him and the buffet tables.

Hawk became aware of Philip coming up behind him. It would look as though Hawk were having a conversation with an old friend's mother and nothing more. Although he'd never heard any whispers about Lady Mattingly's health amongst the *ton,* one could never be too careful.

"Mother, I trust you're finding the evening to your satisfaction."

"Oh, most certainly not, but we're expected to be here, aren't we?" She gestured with her glass. "Your father hasn't stopped carousing at the card tables. You would think he would congratulate the bride to be." Her tone had turned suddenly acerbic, and Hawk smiled harder.

"Perhaps he doesn't wish to ruin the gaiety. What with being the stodgy, old uncle and all." He tried for a note of fun in his voice, but Lady Mattingly frowned with greater force.

"Philip, have you seen Caroline?" she asked as though she had been looking for the girl on the buffet tables.

"She went to get some fresh air, I'm afraid. You know how busy she has been helping Audrey with the wedding planning," Philip said.

Hawk had forgotten she'd been helping Audrey with the wedding planning, but now Caroline's erratic behavior suddenly made more sense. Perhaps she was overwrought, having to help her cousin with the wedding, the same cousin Caroline saw as abandoning her. Maybe that was all tonight's attempted assignation was. A result of the tension and strife Caroline was enduring just then.

He felt some of the weight shift along his shoulders, but there was still more he didn't know. Why was she so determined never to marry? What, if anything, did it have to do with Lady Mattingly's quietude?

"Fresh air?" Lady Mattingly snorted. "That's what all young ladies say when really they are frolicking for a tryst."

Hawk nearly cracked a tooth as he ground his teeth together to keep from speaking.

"Mother." Philip's tone was unforgiving.

"Hello, Lady Mattingly."

Hawk turned at the welcomed sound of a new voice to the mix to find Philip's aunt, Lady Verity, approaching them. Hawk never missed the dark smudges under the woman's eyes, nor the way she seemed colorless and flat. But she smiled, and it was warm and inviting, and Hawk faced another torrent of questions.

He was going to suffer a headache soon if he didn't extract himself from the web of the Hodge family relations.

"Lady Verity," he said with a bow when Philip's mother made no acknowledgment of the woman's greeting. "I trust Grandmother Regina is well seen to."

"Yes, Audrey is with her," Lady Verity assured them with a nod.

Hawk forced a smile to his lips. Audrey? Where had Caroline gone? Had she made it back to the house?

He shouldn't care. He shouldn't worry that she'd been accosted in the garden because he'd left her like the scoundrel she accused him of being.

If anything had happened to her...

He forced the thought away. There was nothing more he could endure that evening, and in fact, the whole of it was growing to be too much. He must excuse himself and get out of there. Distance would be sure to clear his mind.

He opened his mouth to bid everyone good evening when Lady Verity interrupted. "Philip, I would actually like a word if you have a moment."

Hawk paused. In all the years he'd known the Hodge family, Lady Verity had spoken not more than a handful of words. She was more a fixture at Grandmother Regina's side than anything.

"Of course, Aunt Verity, what is it?" Philip responded, but Lady Verity slid a glance in Lady Mattingly's direction.

Hawk interceded. "Lady Mattingly, I do believe Caroline was asking after you. Perhaps she's still on the terrace."

Lady Mattingly's eyebrows went up, but oddly the rest of her face didn't move. She said nothing as she left, her gown billowing on her thin body, the only sign of life about her person.

When she had departed, Lady Verity stepped closer, lowered her voice. "I'm very sorry, Philip, but I thought you would like to know before discovering so yourself."

If Hawk had been tense before, he very much feared he would snap in two now.

"What is it?" Philip's tone matched Lady Verity's.

The poor woman seemed torn between delivering her news and preventing Philip from learning whatever it was. In the end, it seemed prudence won out.

"Philip, I'm afraid Lady Winnaretta is here. She's come to give her good wishes to Audrey. Audrey wished to come tell you herself, but...."

Philip swallowed. Hawk could see it, and it looked painful.

Lady Winnaretta was here? Had she returned to society then, or was she only here out of respect for Audrey?

Suddenly Hawk's world shrank to a cluttered sphere, and he couldn't breathe. He had to get out of there. Everything he had so carefully constructed was colliding around him. But still, he couldn't leave his friend. Not now. Hawk gritted his teeth, but it needn't matter.

Because Philip turned and disappeared through the servants' exit.

6

The day of Audrey's wedding dawned bright and clear.

The birds were chirping some merry tune, the sun was warm across the gardens, and even the breeze was lovely and caressing.

Damn it all.

She wanted it to pour buckets of water from the sky. She wanted a vicious wind to tear at gentlemen's hats and ladies' skirts. She wanted—

She wanted Audrey to have the perfect day.

Meanwhile Caroline was free to nurse her sour, despondent heart.

She hadn't meant to feel this way about her dearest friend being wed, but truly she'd never pictured Audrey marrying. This made her feel like the worst kind of person. But because she hadn't thought of it, she hadn't prepared herself for how she might feel when it happened.

So, when she watched Audrey marry Dash something had welled up inside of her. Something big and unwieldy, pushing at her insides as if to push everything else out to make room for itself. And it was suffocating her.

She drew a deep breath and smiled, brightly, painfully, and nodded at the guests who passed her on the way into the wedding breakfast.

Aunt Eugenia had overdone it on the decorations. It was the one aspect Audrey had given her mother full control over, and it seemed the woman had let it go to her head.

But the guests didn't seem to mind or if they did, they kept their voices low enough Caroline did not hear the complaints.

Audrey and Dash sat at the head table at the other end of the room, their heads already bent together. For one absurd moment, it appeared as though a beam of sunlight shone through the window specifically on them, illuminating them like angels in a Renaissance painting.

She blinked and turned away.

She was allowing her sadness to get the better of her, and she wouldn't stand for it.

Audrey was married now, and that was just the state of things. Caroline could be happy for her cousin or be miserable for the remainder of her life.

While she didn't particularly feel the need to be cheerful, she did decide she would like to be less grumpy and perhaps enjoy the food.

She scanned the table that had been set and found Aunt Eugenia attempting some kind of order, her hands waving madly in the air. If she had thought the guests would file into the room according to titled order, she was mistaken. It seemed the air itself vibrated with anticipation and a lightness the Hodge family hadn't felt in years. Not since before the war.

Caroline was sure the others felt it as well, and because

of such a sense of freedom, they filtered into the room as they saw fit.

Audrey and Dash's immediate family occupied the head table with them, which left Caroline scanning the places at the table for her spot. Audrey had likely placed her next to Philip, and she looked forward to spending a few hours in her brother's company.

Only she didn't find her seat next to Philip.

She found it next to Hawk.

Caroline immediately thought of murdering Audrey, but then she realized that wouldn't be nice on the woman's wedding day. Perhaps another day.

She took her seat before Hawk could appear and pull out her chair for her. She sat quickly, tucking her feet under the chair as if to hold on to it through sheer will. Casually she looked about.

It wasn't that she'd been avoiding Hawk the last couple of weeks. It was just that her time had been spoken for. The wedding was quite a bit to plan, and every spare moment she'd had, she'd given to Audrey. Looking about the room now, Caroline was rather pleased with their results.

It was a grand affair but not overstated. Tasteful and not lavish. Everything that someone like Audrey deserved.

All at once Caroline was overcome by a sense of rightness, and her gaze flew to the bride and groom at the head of the table. Audrey was laughing at something Dash had just said, and the perfection of the moment overwhelmed her.

She had tried not to think about her humiliation that night in the garden with Hawk. She had tried not to consider how her body had betrayed her, but more how the encounter had weakened her resolve. There were moments when Hawk could utterly devastate her with a single word, and yet he consistently reignited the irritation she felt toward him.

Why did the man continue to be so vexing?

As though reading her thoughts, the very man himself sat down next to her at that moment.

An agitated noise slipped through her lips, and Hawk looked swiftly at her, eyebrows raised.

Her cheeks flamed, and she pressed a hand to her mouth.

Slowly a smile came to Hawk's lips as if he were trying to hold back a laugh. "I truly have the most unfortunate effect on you."

She drew a breath, the retort at the ready, but something stopped her. Perhaps it was the vibrations of the day, the merriment around her, the smile on Audrey's face, the way Dash looked at her so adoringly. She would never know what it was, but instead of admonishing him, she smiled.

"I would like to call a truce."

She wasn't sure which of them was more surprised by her words. Hawk seemed to choke, coughing into his hand before saying, "I'm sorry?"

She nodded as if reassuring herself. "I'd like to broker a truce. For one day." She gestured in the direction of the head table. "For Audrey and Dash. It's their special day, and the least we can do is act civilly toward one another."

He leaned back in his chair as if to study her. "You have never been one for diplomacy, Lady Caroline."

She had the rebuke on her lips, but she closed her eyes, willing herself to behave. "That may be, but I believe everyone is capable of change."

"Are they?" He tilted his head in question.

She knew what he was doing. He was attempting to raise

her ire, and she wouldn't let him win. It was his mistake if he underestimated her.

She wasn't sure why she did it, but she reached a hand under the table, wrapping her fingers around his thigh. She took an immeasurable amount of joy in watching his face transform at her daring touch. His eyes tightened, as if he tried not to look down at where her hand lay, his mouth compressing into a thin line, his jaw turning to stone.

"I can be very diplomatic when the situation calls for it, Lord Stonegate."

Her eyes flashed to her hand, sitting so quietly on his thigh, and suddenly she felt sick. She snatched her hand away.

"Why do you always cause me to do things I normally wouldn't?" she hissed, her eyes darting around the table to see if anyone was watching them.

No one was, but it didn't make her feel any less shameful.

She expected him to gloat or at least mock her with a sarcastic grin. But he did none of those things. Instead he swallowed, swallowed so hard she heard it, and turned away from her, picking up his napkin from the place setting on the table. She tried not to watch him, but she couldn't tear her eyes away. It was as though she were waiting for his reaction, preparing herself for the attack, but it never came.

His hands shook as he unfolded his napkin and laid it in his lap, and still, he did not look at her. She wondered for a moment if Hawk had suddenly been replaced by someone else. This was hardly the man she despised. The man off of whom her insults bounced so merrily.

For Hawkins Savage was clearly affected by her just then.

"I'm sorry for that," he said finally, his voice so low it was almost lost in the melee around them.

He'd apologized. He'd apologized to her.

She closed her eyes, turning away from him, as she tried to gather her senses.

"Hawk," she said, her throat dry. "I do truly mean it. About the truce, that is." She poured her earnestness into her voice, but still, he did not look at her. "I would really like us to get along. At least for today."

When he did finally look at her, she was taken aback by the starkness in his eyes. She had never seen such depth in them, such sorrow, and she wondered if she had put it there. That was ridiculous. Hawk didn't care about her or her feelings. She was simply Philip's irritating little sister.

But just then the look on his face told otherwise.

It was as though she had run him cleanly through the heart with a sharp dagger.

"I would like that too. Very much." His voice was nothing as she had heard it before. It was hollow and wistful all at once as if he couldn't believe she would hold to her word.

She felt a sudden pang of regret for all the insults she had hurtled at him, but that was ridiculous. Hawk had always given as good as he had got, and she shouldn't feel even a measure of regret.

But just then she did. It was consuming, this sense that she had let time slip by her. That she had missed something that was right in front of her the whole time.

Her heart thudded in her chest, and a weighty sense of foreboding pressed down on her. There was something brewing between them. Something she knew could only end in an explosion, and she only hoped that neither of them would be hurt.

She couldn't stop the image of her mother, broken and

betrayed, from springing to her mind, but instead of letting it linger, she shoved it away. Today was a day of hope and happiness, and she was not going to allow the memory to take over.

She forced a smile, one that felt too bright, but it was a start. "Then we should start right now." She placed her hands in her lap with determination. "Hello, Lord Stonegate, you look fine today."

The words were ludicrous, and a laugh burst from her lips before she could stop it. Hawk studied her, a wary expression on his features before his face relaxed into a tentative smile.

"Why thank you, Lady Caroline. Your flattery is much appreciated."

She frowned. "You take that as flattery?"

Hawk laughed. "It's the nicest thing you've said to me since you first laid eyes on me."

"I suppose that's true."

She was prevented from saying more when Dash suddenly appeared at Hawk's elbow, leaning conspiratorially over the back of Hawk's chair.

"Aren't you supposed to be with your bride?" she said quickly.

Dash smiled but it lacked the warmth she would expect from the groom on his wedding day. Tension sprang to her shoulders, fear instantly gripping her.

This was what happened. She'd let her guard down once, and everything crumbled.

Her eyes flashed from Dash to Hawk.

"May I speak with you?" Dash asked, his tone low.

"Anything you must say to him, you can say to me." The words flew from her lips before she could stop them, and she knew how unreasonable she sounded.

She had no right to intercede in a conversation between Dash and Hawk. They were old friends, and what they had to say to one another was no concern of hers. But she couldn't shake the feeling that what Dash had to say was something she would not enjoy.

Hawk considered her before turning to Dash. "I suppose you can be out with it. Lady Caroline is already privy to far too much that occurs between the three of us," he said referring to the friendship that had started in their school days between Dash, Hawk, and Philip.

Dash eyed Caroline warily, and she straightened in her seat, her hands fisting in her lap.

Dash swallowed and turned back to Hawk. Very carefully he spoke. "Audrey has just told me about the engagement ball."

Caroline's cheeks flamed, and involuntarily she shot to her feet, knocking her elbow into her plate, cracking it into the crystal, and drawing everyone's attention to her.

"What about the engagement ball?" She was causing a scene. She could feel everyone's eyes on her, and a sharp stab of guilt pierced her.

She was ruining Audrey's day, but her world continued to tilt out of balance, and she was desperate to right it.

How did Dash know about their encounter in the garden that night? For that matter, how had Audrey known? Caroline hadn't told a soul.

Caroline's eyes flew about the room. She found Pippa in the seat farthest from everyone else, Lady Spader nodding off beside her. But Pippa wasn't looking at her. She was one of the few people who weren't. But it was only because Gavin, Audrey's brother, had captured Pippa's attention.

Dash looked only at Hawk as he said, "I meant about Lady Winnaretta."

Caroline's body went entirely cold. Her heart stopped thudding. Her hands uncurled. She licked her lips and whispered, "What about Lady Winnaretta?"

Dash's glance slid between Hawk and her, and her stomach rolled.

She stepped forward, nearly colliding with Hawk who was still sitting.

"What about Lady Winnaretta?" Her voice rose. She couldn't stop it.

Vaguely she saw Audrey's other brother, Ethan, separate himself from the crowd, his face a mask of stone.

But before Ethan could do anything, Dash answered. "She was at the engagement ball, Caroline. It appears she's returned to society."

She was drowning. She was drowning all over again just as she had been that day in the pond, but now she stood on solid ground. She didn't wait for anything further.

She turned and fled.

H<small>E FOLLOWED HER.</small>

He knew her well enough to imagine the turmoil coursing through her. He wasn't surprised by her mad dash from the wedding breakfast. In fact, he had already been reaching for her when she'd turned and all but ran for the door.

He couldn't sprint after her. She would never survive the rumors such an action would cause. But he could slip into the bustle she left in her wake as Audrey's brother, Baron Grays, stepped forward to call order to the room with a toast to the bride and groom.

The guests, keen for a new distraction now that Caroline

had left, were all too eager to turn their eyes to the head table. Hawk swept the room quickly before slipping through the door, but Philip was nowhere to be found. Where had the man gone off to? It should be he who comforted Caroline now. It was far too dangerous for Hawk to attempt it, and yet, he found himself climbing the stairs of Dartford House, following the retreating sound of her footsteps on the floor above.

He was unfamiliar with Dartford House, but Caroline's stampeding retreat was loud enough for him to ascertain the way she had gone. He rounded the landing on the floor above where the guests were and strode down the corridor, passing a startled maid holding a stack of towels as if she planned to use it to defend herself. As the poor woman was also pressed against the wall, Hawk took that to mean Caroline had passed through there at a steady pace.

He nodded to the poor servant with a warm smile, but she only blinked at him, her fingers pressing into the towels.

He rounded the corner at the end of the corridor just as a door on the right clicked shut.

He should have stopped. He should have left her alone. But he couldn't. Quite simply he couldn't. Something inside of him drove him to her, but he couldn't have said whether it was to provide explanation or comfort or both.

He pushed through the door without knocking and closed it quickly behind him, sending the lock home.

"What are you doing?" Her voice was as cold as he'd ever heard it, but it was the tinge of hysteria in it that had his chest tightening.

"Despite my actions of late, I do care about your reputation, and I do not wish for someone to come upon us unexpectedly."

He'd given her little time to do more than walk into the

room, and she stood there now, her arms loose at her sides, looking all the world as if she were lost.

And she was lost.

He understood that. Everything about her world continued to suffer upheaval, and he couldn't do anything to make that better. But he knew, he *knew* it was this upheaval of which she was most afraid.

He moved to step toward her and froze. He had expected her to flee to one of the family drawing rooms. He knew from experience that the Hodge cousins tended to flit from each other's homes, and it wouldn't be unusual for Caroline to seek out the comfort of a familiar drawing room. But this wasn't that.

This was a bedroom.

The bed leered at him ominously, and his throat threatened to close off entirely as his lungs already struggled to draw air.

"Where are we?" His voice was hollow to his own ears, and he sensed the edge looming up at him. He had only to step off, and he could take everything he had ever wanted. Carefully he slid his gaze to Caroline, found her standing still so alone in the middle of the carpet.

"My rooms, and I didn't say you could be here." Her tone was strong even if her body appeared fragile.

"You have a room at Dartford House?"

Her fingers flexed but otherwise she didn't move. "Of course I do. Audrey has rooms at Mattingly House as well."

He watched as realization dawned on her, saw the way her eyes widened, her lips parted, and then it was as though her body simply folded. Her hands went to her head as if to hold it while her knees gave way. He caught her, his arms wrapping around her as he pulled her in the direction of the bed.

God, why was there no furniture in this room? Not a sofa or even a chair. He would take a simple chair just then. Caroline was slight and could easily fit on his lap—

He looked at the ceiling, sucking in a breath as he tightened his arms around her, held her head beneath his chin. He had to remain the gentleman here. He was only there to provide comfort.

"Caroline," he whispered, stroking her hair from her face.

She shook now, but he thought that was from fear and not tears.

"Audrey's never going to stay in that room again, is she?" Her voice carried the whole of her despair, and it twisted like a knife in his gut.

He pressed his lips to her forehead, unable to stop himself. "She will. She will stay in that room only she'll have Dash with her now, and God willing, one day they may come with their children. Wouldn't that be wonderful? Wouldn't you like to see Audrey's children?"

She shook against him, her entire body vibrating against his, and he held her tighter, his lips traveling to her temple.

"Why must everything change?" she whispered, her fingers curling into his jacket.

He leaned back far enough to put a bent finger under her chin and lift her face to his.

"Change isn't always for the worse, pet," he said and pressed a kiss to her lips.

He thought she would resist him, push him away, even slap him, but she didn't. She reached for him, with her body, with her soul, with everything she had. He could feel it, the way she yearned to him, wrapping her arms around him, and lifting her face to his kiss.

He had to stop. He had only ever taken her like this in a

state of tension and despair and turmoil, and he didn't wish to do it again. He didn't like that she only responded to him like this when her mind was muddled. When she was thinking clearly, she remembered how much she hated him and attacked him with words and coldness.

But this Caroline was different. This Caroline clung to him as if he were everything to her, as if he were her very breath.

Why didn't clear-headed Caroline do the same? But more, why did he wish her to? Why did it suddenly matter so much that she know, clearly and distinctly, how she felt about him?

He broke the kiss and surged to his feet, spiking his fingers through his hair as he crossed the room. When he turned back, she was sprawled across the bed where his sudden departure had left her.

"Caroline, I won't do this again. I only came here to see if you were all right. I will not confuse you again."

She pushed herself back into a seated position, her eyes widening. "Confuse me? Is that what you did that night in the garden? Is that what you think happened?"

"You said it yourself not moments ago." He pointed at the floor as if she could see the wedding breakfast. "You said I make you do things you normally wouldn't, and I shan't be guilty of it again."

She stood, wobbling slightly, but she soon steadied herself. He flexed his hands into fists, willing himself not to go to her.

"You think this is your fault? What about me?" She pressed a hand to her chest. "I'm just as guilty as you are, aren't I?"

He shook his head. "It's not how you think it is."

"And how is it precisely?"

"I've always clouded your judgment even before now. Tell me. Have you ever held a single favorable thought about me?"

She blinked, her lips pursing. "Of course I have."

"Tell me what it was."

She blinked again, her mouth opening several times without words. Finally she shook her head. "I can't think clearly right now, but I know there was one."

She took a step toward him, and he took a step back, his hip going into the delicate dressing table behind him. He reached for the mirror as it swung wildly on in its trestle. But Caroline still advanced. He let go of the mirror, allowing it to bang into the wall as he tried to evade her, but there was only so much space in the room.

She had him pinned to the wall when she finally stopped her advance.

"I don't want a husband, Hawk." Her eyes were fiery and her chin sure.

"And I do not wish for a wife." He wasn't sure how that was supposed to stop her. It seemed rather to be more in agreement with her own tastes.

"But I do want a lover."

He heard her words, felt them sink to the depths of his very core, but he couldn't pry his eyes from her lips. They were swollen from his kiss, bright red and plump, begging for his attention.

"You don't want a lover, Caroline. Your reputation—"

"Doesn't matter if I am never to marry."

"You will wish to marry one day, and you will regret this." Roses. Her scent was invading every pore, and he couldn't bear it. He pressed his fingertips into the wall behind him, trying to focus on the imprint of the plaster against his skin, anything to distract himself from her nearness.

"I shall never marry," she said, her face hardening with the words. "I shall never let anyone have such control over me."

Suddenly his mind flashed to Lady Mattingly, drifting aimlessly across the buffet room at the engagement, and he wondered again what had happened. What had Caroline witnessed while Philip had been away at school? And why had it sparked such fastidiousness in Caroline?

"And you think a lover wouldn't have the same outcome?"

Finally she stopped in her advance, her eyes darting from side to side as if considering his words.

"A lover is not legally binding."

"Is that what frightens you? The permanence of it?"

She had never been one to be fickle in nature, and she had time and again displayed her displeasure of change, so why should the formality of marriage frighten her?

"It's not the length of a marriage that I object to. It's the pervasiveness of it."

He studied her face, the passion in her eyes at war with the firmness of her chin. "And you don't think a lover would invade your life with such totality?"

"I wouldn't allow him to." The words were swift and direct, and she never moved her eyes from his.

Her voice burned with determination, and it twisted at something inside of him, but he couldn't pinpoint what. Perhaps it was despair that she should wish to hold herself apart from others, that she should feel the need to take such drastic measures to protect herself.

And yet...

If she didn't wish to entangle herself in emotional trappings, she could take a lover that meant nothing more than the physical aspect of it. It was a dangerous game to play, and he should have warned her of such, but another part of him had awakened to the possibility.

A lover.

A lover with no expectations.

A simple affair of mutual understanding.

He let his mind go, prodding gently at the black void that was his future, but as it did every time he thought of it, he could see nothing past his thirtieth birthday. It would all be over then. It must. For anything else didn't make sense.

But to have an affair with the one woman who had ever captured his heart? To feel her, to taste her, to know her before the end of everything? Knowing in the end, that it was what she wanted?

He had promised to be a gentleman, and a gentleman always obeyed a lady's wish.

"You want a lover," he said, testing the words on his tongue.

She reached up and took him by the lapels of his jacket. "I want you," she said.

"Lovers only." There was no question, and yet he wanted the words spoken aloud, for him or her, he wasn't sure.

"Lovers only," she said.

He didn't waste another moment. He picked her up and carried her to the bed.

7

S omething had passed over his face right before he grabbed her.

Distantly her mind mulled it over even as he laid her on the bed, covering her with his body, and sealing his lips to hers.

Was it relief? Or worse, hope?

She wanted to quiet her mind, but the thought kept invading. Relief from what? Hope for what? It was as though she had released him from a prison of his own making. But how could that be?

All at once the pieces of the puzzle that made him up tumbled about her, and she realized she didn't know who he was at all. The man she had so loved to hate wasn't the person she thought he was. He was a benefactor in his parish, and she knew, somehow, she knew, he was stead-fastly keeping Lady Winnaretta's secret.

The realization came to her in that moment, when she held him in her arms, and as soon as it came, she pushed it away. She didn't want to think about Hawk like that. She didn't want to see him as a caring, considerate, understanding person. If she thought too much of him, she would be in danger of losing her heart to him.

Instead she just wanted to feel. She wanted that lightness, that freedom that came from losing herself in his arms. She wanted him to chase the worry away. She wanted to forget for one moment that she was Philip's sister, that she was her mother's daughter.

His lips nibbled at hers, and she chased his kiss, lifting her head from the pillow only to have him press her into it as he came fully atop her, settling between her legs. Her gown would be ruined, and she'd be unable to return to the wedding breakfast, but she didn't care. She didn't care about anything just then.

Not when his lips left hers, trailing a hot line along her jaw and down to her neck. She arched, opening herself up to him, and only then did she realize his fingers had been busy behind her. The bodice of her gown loosened, and she sucked in a full breath, her fingers digging into his shoulders.

"Hawk."

He didn't answer, his lips traveling the length of her neck to bite playfully at her collarbone. Pleasure, so intense, so focused, shot through her, and she struggled against the confines of her loosened gown.

"Hawk. I must—"

But she didn't have time to say more. He leaned back, and with such strength and contradicting delicacy, he tugged her gown cleanly down her body, finally freeing her legs as he tossed it aside.

She realized with a jolt that he had done this before, and while she felt a spark of alarm, it faded as soon as he returned to her arms. She wouldn't think of it. She didn't wish to think of Hawk's past. Or her past for that matter. She only wanted this, right now, and none of the rest of it should matter.

Left only in her chemise and corset, the rough fabric of his jacket scraped at her bare arms, and she plunged her hands under the lapels, shoving the garment from his shoulders. He helped her, shedding the jacket, his waistcoat, and cravat. It all happened in a matter of seconds as though they were both frantic to have as little as possible between them.

But then he returned to her with a kiss, tracing the outline of her lips, nibbling the corners of her mouth, before resuming his trek down her neck. She lifted herself to him, holding him against her with greedy hands pressed to his back. But it wasn't enough. She wanted to feel him. She wanted to touch the hot skin she knew was there and just out of reach.

He pushed aside the strap of her chemise, his tongue sending a wave of desire rippling through her as he traced the curve of her shoulder. She scrambled, her fingers pulling at his shirt until it was freed of his breeches. The moment her fingers touched his bare skin, he settled his mouth along the top of her breast.

"Hawk." She reared up against him, her body coiling with unbelievable pleasure, a pulsing stirring deep within her. "Hawk, I need—"

But he didn't wait for her to finish. He grasped the hem of her chemise, and with one fluid movement tugged it up to her waist. Much like the gown, the movement was practiced and smooth, and just for a moment, she felt a pang of remorse. But that was silly. She knew exactly who Hawk was, and she shouldn't regret seeing glimpses of his true nature.

Besides, now he could see almost all of her with her

corset raised and her silk stockings the only thing covering her legs.

Suddenly she realized how exposed she was, the thought coming with the abruptness of a splash of cold water.

"Hawk." She let go of him, trying to cover herself, but he captured her hands.

"No, Caroline." His voice was rough, so unlike the cultured tone she was used to, and her heart thudded in response. "I want to see all of you."

He reached out a single fingertip. She thought he would touch her in her most intimate place, bared for him now, but he didn't. Instead his finger found its way to the curve of her hip. He traced it, the rough callus of his fingertip lighting a fire along her skin.

She was transfixed by his touch, but more, by the way he devoured her with his eyes. It was as though she were something rare and precious, and he couldn't have looked away for all the riches in the world.

Something deeper traveled through her then. Something weightier than desire, and for a moment, her throat closed in fear. But then he looked up, met her gaze, and the trepidation fled at the fire she saw there.

This was only about the physical act. Hawk didn't care about her in that way. They had only to assuage their attraction for one another, and they could return to how things had been. An emotional distance that suited them both.

"You're so beautiful."

The words were guttural, and they shook her recently recovered resolve. But no, he didn't mean it like that. He was only attempting to arouse her with pretty words.

"You mustn't say that," she said, her hands reaching for him as he knelt between her legs. "It's not—"

He leaned over her, placing a hand on either side of her head as he leaned down, capturing her gaze with his stormy one.

"I must say it. It's what I've been thinking for so long that if I don't say it, it might kill me." He kissed her with an intensity he hadn't displayed before, and she suddenly forgot his words, her fear, everything.

She wrapped her arms around him, her fingers finding the hem of his shirt and slipping beneath it to trace the corded muscles of his back. His hands ran down her sides, and she cursed her corset, but then he reached her bared hips, and his hands slipped around, cupping her buttocks as he pulled her against him.

The movement opened her up, and she felt him, all of him, hard against her.

She knew how the sexual act worked, but suddenly feeling him sent a bolt of passion clean through her. She knew she should be demure, shy, and reserved, but she felt none of those things. The feel of him—God, he was so hard—was unlike anything she had expected, and suddenly she wanted him with a fervor so intense it took her breath.

She reached for the front of his breeches, her fingers fumbling against the buttons. He placed his hand over hers, stilling her fingers.

"Not yet," he murmured against her neck, and then he was gone.

He slid down her body out of her reach, and she lifted her head from the pillow, watching him.

He pressed his mouth to her thigh, just above the edge of her stocking. Heat built inside of her at his touch, but something had changed, shifted. It was as though her body had suddenly become alive, all her nerve endings tingling in awareness. She watched him, mesmerized, as he moved his lips up the inside of her thigh.

Oh God, he was going to put his mouth...there.

Her fingers curled into the bedclothes, her eyes unable to look away, and then—

Bliss.

Her head fell back to the pillow as her eyes closed in tormented desire. She dug her heels into the mattress, lifting herself, offering her body to him. He gripped her hips, his tongue flicking her sensitive nub with teasing strokes before he settled his mouth against her, the heat and sensation nearing unbearable pleasure.

"Hawk." She tried to squirm under his torturous machinations, but he held her still with his big hands, pinning her to the mattress.

The pleasure built, focused, and then when it exploded, she came up off the mattress, a silent scream parting her lips.

She collapsed against the bed, but he kept his mouth still against her as the echoes of her pleasure dissipated.

"Hawk." Her voice was weak and pitiful now, her body sapped of tension.

He had done this to her. He had taken away the ever-present worry, the constant feeling of dread. He had taken everything away, leaving her to feel nothing but the pleasure of her own body.

Slowly he drew atop her, and dimly she heard the rustling of fabric, and then he was pressed against her. All of him.

And he was even bigger than she had imagined. Her eyes flew to the place where they were joined, and she didn't know how it was possible, but the pleasure began to build inside of her once again.

"Hawk, are you sure…" But she didn't know the question she was asking.

He cupped her face in his hands, leaning on his elbows over her.

"I'm very sure," he said, answering a question she hadn't asked, and she wondered if he thought her unsure.

But she wasn't. She shifted, lifting her hips to open herself to him, to show him how sure she was about her decision, how much she wanted this, wanted *him*.

He moved between her legs, shifting, prodding.

He groaned, his eyes closing. "Oh God, you're so wet."

As if her body understood his words, she clenched, her muscles responding to his exploring fingers. And then he pushed inside of her.

He filled her, and while she had expected pain, it wasn't that so much as an adjusting, her body expanding around him.

And then…pleasure.

It roared inside of her, her heart racing, her lips parting as she tried to suck in a breath.

Her world tilted then, coming to a sudden point where it was only she and Hawk. The rest of it fell away, and she couldn't understand how anything else had existed before then.

He began to move, sliding into her completely before pulling back. Her desire spun, twisting and coiling, and the heat built within her.

"Oh God, Hawk." She clawed at his shoulders, trying to bring herself closer to him.

He took her mouth in a hot kiss as he tortured her with his slow, even thrusts. Each one sent a bolt of pleasure through her, and she wanted. She wanted something just out of reach.

"Hawk, please," she cried against his lips.

Only then did he begin to move faster, his hips slamming into her. The pleasure grew to an unbearable point, but it was as though her body held herself back for him. She could feel his own pleasure mounting as his body tightened under her hands. He ripped his mouth from hers, his head going back, jaw taut.

"Hawk, I need." She needed everything. She needed him. All of him. Right then.

He seemed to understand because he reached down and flicked a single finger over her sensitive nub. She exploded, pleasure tearing through her until she could no longer hold herself up, hold Hawk against her.

But she felt his release on the edge of hers, and together they tumbled.

A PARTICULARLY BOISTEROUS cheer from below jolted him back to reality, and with it the crushing reality of where they were.

Or rather where he was.

He pushed up on his elbows, his gaze drifting down the length of them as if he couldn't quite believe what had just happened. But it had.

He had made love to Caroline. His best friend's little sister. His archenemy. The woman he loved so completely. He wasn't sure what vexed him more.

But her eyes opened, sleepily, and a contented smile appeared on her lips.

And he couldn't give a damn if she was his archenemy or his best friend's little sister or anything else.

She was his.

The thought thundered through him, and he felt it ring clear down to his toes.

Which were still nestled in his boots.

Dear God, he hadn't even gotten fully undressed.

The manic that had consumed him at the first idea of taking her as a lover receded now, and with it came a clarity that was not altogether comforting.

He had ruined her. He wanted to care more that he had done it, but even as he scolded himself, he couldn't help but feel a bit of wonder and pride. He had *ruined* her, but it still felt more like he had *claimed* her.

Something sharp and painful twisted in his chest, and he knew it was the sense of permanency that such an idea suggested.

Caroline wasn't his to have forever. Nothing was. Yet he had taken her, and everything that entailed at the first suggestion of it.

If she had not told him she would not wed, would he have still done it?

If she had not been so adamant in her denial of wishing for a wedded future, would he still have taken her innocence?

No.

He felt the word like a brick falling in his stomach, and once more, he wanted to hate himself. But he couldn't.

He couldn't hate anything when he studied the sleepy, satisfied face beneath his.

"Is it always like that?" she whispered without opening her eyes.

He reached up and brushed a strand of her golden hair from her forehead. "No." He was whispering too, although he couldn't say why. The awe of the moment or the gravity of the situation. "Sometimes it's better."

Her eyes flew open at this, indignation in her gaze.

He laughed and kissed her temple. "As we learn each other's bodies, understand what the other likes, it will get even better."

He shouldn't have said it. A curiousness passed over her eyes then, and her fingers clenched against his back.

He tugged himself free of her grasp even before she could speak.

"But not now, pet. Not now." He laughed as he extracted himself. "Later. There will be time later to explore each other."

He gained his feet, quickly covering himself. Not for her sensibilities, but he suddenly realized how easily they could be discovered. He looked up to find her still sprawled across the bed, naked except for her corset and stockings, her chemise shoved to her hips, and the very image of her was enough to have him hardening again. He turned away, searching for his discarded jacket and cravat.

He heard her sit up behind him, but he kept his mind focused on his task, willing his body to calm.

He had never allowed himself to dream of what it would be like to make love to Caroline. He had never permitted himself the luxury. But he was finding the reality of it was far greater than any dream he might have conjured.

She was eager and curious, not at all the diminutive debutante her station would have suggested. But he could have guessed as much. There was nothing about Caroline that was in any way quiet or demure. That was likely why he had found himself attracted to her in the first place.

He heard a rustling behind him and finally allowed himself to turn as he shrugged into his waistcoat and jacket. She had donned a dressing gown, and that fateful day at the house party came soaring back to him. He couldn't stop his eyes from traveling to her feet, her stockinged toes pressed into the carpets.

He had promised to stay away from her. He shouldn't have stolen what he had that day, and now look where he was. The agony of his future pierced him then, slaying the golden glow from lovemaking that still hung between them. His gaze drifted upward, taking in every inch of her as if she were the last beautiful thing he would ever see.

For she was.

It was hard to breathe then, his chest twisting, his heart racing, and all he could do was study her. This beautiful creature who against all odds wanted him.

Even as the thought formed, he felt the niggle of suspicion. She wanted him, yes, but not all of him, and this brought a sensation of incompleteness.

Despair and sadness washed over him, and he instantly rejected the feeling. Not today. Not now. He didn't want to think of anything that would tarnish this moment. This was one of so few happy moments he would have. He didn't wish for anything to taint it.

He stepped forward and tugged her into his arms. Her hair had fallen loose from its intricate knotting, and as he pulled her close, he buried his hands in her mane. She tilted her head back, ready for his kiss, but he didn't kiss her. He only studied her face, massaged the nape of her neck, and only then, finally, did he lean down and press a gentle kiss to her lips.

Her arms had gone around his back, and at the touch of his lips, her fingers pressed into him. The moment spun out as if it would last forever, and in his mind, he suddenly pictured it.

A moment like this, many moments like this, of standing in his bedchamber, Caroline in his arms. He could picture it so clearly, and then it began to evolve, spinning in a revolution around his mind. This same moment, Caroline's hair loose around his shoulders, her dressing gown the only thing separating them. The smell of fresh air and horse as if he had just returned from a long ride to find his wife waiting for him.

Wife.

He released her as though he'd been shocked, and quite frankly it felt like he had. His skin tingled, and he busied himself with tying his cravat to keep his hands from shaking.

He had never had a thought to his future. Not before now. Not before this. It had always been an empty, black void, and that was how he knew his life would end on his thirtieth birthday four weeks from then.

But now he had Caroline. He had tasted her, felt her, and she had become real and pervasive like she never had before.

He didn't allow himself to think of what this meant or how it made him feel. It was just an aberration. As she had said herself, they were satisfying a physical urge and nothing more.

He had to remember that.

But even as he firmed his resolve, the image that sprung into his mind, fully formed, refused to go away.

"And when is it that we'll have such time to learn each other as you so put it?"

He looked up sharply at her question. She had come closer, following him in the direction of the door, her hands playing with the loose tie of her gown. He could see her corset through the parted lapel, and his gaze traveled up to the heave of her breasts.

He hadn't even touched them, tasted them, explored

them. There was so much left of Caroline that he had yet to enjoy, and once again, his future opened like a chasm of rock splintering to reveal a vast cavern of sparkling crystals.

He blinked and forced himself to focus. She didn't want a future, and he didn't have one. He wouldn't allow his mind to play tricks on him.

"In case you've forgotten I'm an unmarried young lady. It's not as though I can be seen entering your house." She gestured around them. "And it's also not as though we have a wedding breakfast to sneak away from every day."

Her tone was practical, and her face had taken on a familiar look. He was usually at the receiving end of such a look for some perceived misdeed, and it was pleasant to realize he was not the subject of her annoyance at the moment. But rather their situation was.

He stepped forward and took her shoulders into his hands. "I promise you I will arrange for a discreet meeting. No one will know about it."

Her frown was swift and fierce. "I'm not so much worried about the discovery of our affair but rather how long it will be until you can arrange such a meeting." She played with the folds of his cravat, laying the fabric in proper contours. "I shouldn't like to wait too long."

His body clenched, anticipation thrumming through his veins. He laid his forehead against hers. "I should not like to wait too long either."

He wanted to kiss her again, but he didn't trust himself. He eased her away, but she kept her grip on him.

"How do I know you're telling the truth?" Her voice had gone quiet and soft, and he wondered for a moment if she was starting to regret what they had done.

"Of course I'm telling the truth." He put a finger under

her chin to lift her gaze to his. "Do you think me capable of treating you with such a cavalier attitude?"

Her eyes widened. "I wasn't aware you knew such big words, my lord." Her grin was mocking.

"I assure you, pet. My vocabulary is quite robust."

While he had expected to see a responding fire in her eyes at his use of her pet name, he was surprised to see her features quiet and become reflective. She reached up a hand and cupped his cheek.

"I rather don't mind that name any longer actually," she said, and her tone suggested she was as surprised as he was.

Something shifted between them. Something tantamount and dangerous, and it was as if both were realizing it at the same time, each heavily aware of the other. If he were the fanciful sort, he would have said it was their past moving between them, transforming as it took on a new dimension.

Suddenly he wondered if she would realize the truth of his part in her brother's near ruin. But that was ridiculous. She still didn't know the truth, and with the thought, he remembered what had made her flee the wedding breakfast in the first place.

"Caroline, about Lady Winnaretta..." He didn't know what he was going to say, but he suddenly felt the need to assure her before he left. "I can't say why she's returned to society, but I would caution you not to think more of it. We can't know that she's come to find Philip again."

Her eyes widened as she took him in. "Do you think she would seek Philip out?"

Tension gripped him. "Is that not what you believed?"

She shook her head. "I was only worried that she might cause Philip's reputation further harm by appearing in society. Not that she would seek him out directly." She pulled herself from his grip. "Why would she want to see Philip? I thought...all of that business was over."

He noticed her pause, the way her eyes drifted to the carpet as if she couldn't speak the words.

"Do you mean their broken engagement?"

Her eyes flashed to his. "Yes. Precisely." She licked her lips. Nervously? Agitatedly?

Once more he couldn't help but remember Lady Mattingly's ghostlike stroll across the buffet room at the engagement ball, and something moved within him, something that didn't quite fit the rest of the picture Caroline showed the world.

He stepped forward and cupped her chin. "All of that business is finished, pet. You mustn't worry over it." He kissed her, briefly, softly, just enough to distract her without allowing them to fall back into each other's arms.

He broke away and took purposeful strides toward the door. "I must go before we're discovered. Promise me you'll not try something foolish."

She tilted her head, her eyes innocent. "When have I ever done anything foolish?"

He didn't bother with a response and released the lock on the door before turning back to her. "Lock this after me. Who knows what kind of wastrels are in attendance downstairs," he said with a grin and slipped out.

8

Perhaps if Audrey hadn't left for her wedding trip, and if the weather had been more favorable instead of boxing her inside with its days of unending rain, she may have kept her word to Hawk.

But as boredom crept along the last of her nerves, she gave up.

Well, gave up was rather a strong way to think of it as she hadn't tried very hard in the first place to do as Hawk bid.

Not that she would tell him that as the hackney drew to a stop at the end of the alley running along the backside of the row of townhomes where Hawk resided.

She alighted and paid the driver before turning down the alleyway. She hadn't thought about how dark it would be. Or how the cavernous path would ring with the sounds of the inhabitants who lived along it. She heard the ping of a hammer against a horseshoe somewhere in the darkness and wondered why a blacksmith would be working in the mews at this hour, but then if his master wished to depart at first light, there was no other time for it, was there?

She dodged the puddles she could see, but unfortunately her slippers did not survive the trip entirely, her feet slipping into unseen debris and damp. By the time she found the rear entrance of Hawk's residence, she was quite eager to get indoors.

She had never attempted anything quite this daring, and really she hadn't thought it at all perilous. But the cover of night changed things, making sinister what in the daylight would be mundane.

She slipped through the back gate, her eyes falling on the quiet mews. The rear yard held a smattering of wandering chickens, already headed in the direction of what appeared to be their roost as she entered, her arrival only making them scurry more for their safe nests.

When she reached the wooden door set into the basement of the towering townhome, she froze.

She hadn't really thought of this bit.

Was she simply to announce herself? What would the servants think? Surely someone would talk.

"Have you lost your senses?"

She whirled at the guttural voice behind her, but before she could fully turn, hands like iron bands descended on her shoulders, spinning her about until she was well and captured.

Hawk's glare was intense enough to pierce the darkness.

She licked her lips. "I do apologize. I did try to behave."

He growled instead of responding and reached for the hood of her cloak, pulling it roughly over her head.

"Keep your head down and for God's sake, don't say anything."

He didn't give her a chance to reply. He wrenched open the door and strode in, pulling her unceremoniously behind him. She did as he bid, keeping her eyes toward the floor. Although she couldn't help a peek or two as he led her through what must have been the kitchens, still bustling even at this late hour as servants readied the food for the next day. A maid churned milk in the dairy room while another kneaded dough at a wooden table in the next. They passed a pair of footmen carving cheeses and what appeared to be a roast of beef.

But they were through before she could see more, and he pushed her ahead of him along what appeared to be a servant's staircase. The space was cramped but well lit, unusual for a servant's entrance, and she wondered once again just who Hawk was when she wasn't busy scolding him.

They emerged on the upper floor in a quiet, dimly lit corridor. Hawk didn't pause, sweeping up her hand and tugging her down the hallway.

She lost count of the number of doors they passed or the direction in which they were going as he turned corner after corner before pulling her through a door, shutting it soundly behind her.

She was plunged into darkness, the room about her a mystery. Absently she realized she held her breath, listening for the sounds of Hawk moving about in the blackness. As her eyes adjusted, she found the orange glow of a banked fire what seemed a distance into the room, but that was all.

Finally there was the strike of a match and a soft light appeared. She could just make out the shade of a lantern as Hawk replaced it on the now burning wick. He adjusted the flame, and soft yellow light spilled across the floor. She took in the intricate weavings of the lush carpet at her feet, the edging detail of a fine hardwood desk, and—

Books.

There were books everywhere. Piles on the floor, on tables and chairs, and the desk. By the time her eyes took it all in, Hawk had lit another lantern, and more light flooded the room. Her gaze swept upward, to the overflowing shelves that disappeared into the darkness at the ceiling.

She wasn't sure how long she stood there in silence, studying the room about her, but when she finally sought out Hawk, she found him watching her, brooding silently as he leaned back against the desk.

"Find anything of interest?"

She still wore her hood pulled low on her brow, and she shoved it carelessly from her head. "Who is reading all these books?"

"I am." His tone was neutral, and this more than anything piqued her curiosity.

"All of them? Whatever for? Do you think you'll never get through them?"

She wished the light had been better because something passed over his face then, much as it had done the other day when she had convinced him to become her lover. There was more to Hawk than he presented to the world, and she was ashamed she was only discovering it now.

"I didn't know you enjoyed reading," she said softly, regret weakening her words.

"You never asked." Again his tone was neutral, but still she flinched at what his words suggested.

She moved carefully into the room, touching the spine of the uppermost book on a stack by the sofa.

"What are you doing here?" he asked.

The instinct to prod him about the curious look that had passed over his face was strong, but she had other matters she intended to see to that night. She squared her shoulders. "We have an agreement if you recall."

He raised an eyebrow. "And what is that?"

She became aware he was dressed for the evening. He

must have been out when he caught her at the door, and she frowned. She hadn't thought he might be out. She had rather suspected he would be at home, pining for her. How incredibly selfish that thought was, but then several questions flooded her at once.

"Where were you?"

He blinked. "I don't see how that's relevant."

Her eyes widened. "Are you keeping secrets? How unlike you."

The jab was unnecessary and childish, and she rather regretted it. The old Caroline would have made such a petty overture, but she truly wished they were beyond that now.

She held up a hand. "I'm sorry. I'm finding it difficult adjusting to our new roles." She smiled, hoping he'd understand.

He crossed his arms over his chest, but he returned her smile as he said, "I was with Philip if you must know. But seeing as you are here, you must know Philip was not home and taken advantage of his absence."

She couldn't help it when her smile turned into a grin. "Philip would have been the only one to notice if I had slipped out. It was rather good of him to go out this evening." She frowned again. "Where had he gone exactly?"

Hawk pushed away from the desk, shucking his greatcoat as he made his way behind it. "Poking your nose where it doesn't belong again, pet? I thought you had outgrown that."

"I will never outgrow my curiosity," she said, reaching for the ties of her cloak. "How is one to gain knowledge if she loses her curiosity?"

"Read a book," he said flatly. He deposited his coat on the ponderous leather chair behind the desk before moving to a side table. He picked up a decanter and a glass, gesturing to her. "It's whiskey, but somehow I think you should like to try it."

She wrinkled her nose. "I've already tried it actually and find it not to my liking."

He blinked again. "You've already tried it?"

Caroline nodded, slipping the cloak from her shoulders as she studied the room. The books continued, piling on surfaces across the room. Tables were scattered here and there. Some held chairs pushed to their sides while others contained only the piles of books.

"Audrey and I stole some of Father's years ago. Dreadful stuff." She turned back in time to see Hawk's grin.

He poured a glass and then another, bringing one to her.

"I think perhaps you should try it again. You may find your tastes have...changed." The last word carried a meaningful hesitation, and she met his gaze directly.

"I'm finding many of my tastes have changed of late." She accepted the proffered glass. "I will take your suggestion."

She sipped delicately at the liquor. Warmth hit her first, and after her adventure down the alleyway, she welcomed the heat. She was surprised by the subtle tones that followed, the woody taste that lingered on her tongue.

He had turned away from her, making his way back to the desk, and she was glad he couldn't see her reaction to the whiskey.

Enough had changed already. It wouldn't do for something so simple as her tastes to have changed as well.

She set down the glass, careful not to upset the pile of books perched on the edge of the table before wandering deeper into the room.

"I wouldn't have taken you for a lover of books," she said, fingering the worn leather cover of a book of sonnets.

Sonnets?

She turned to face him, but he didn't seem keen on answering her.

She made her way back to him. It wasn't important that she get to know Hawk in that way. To learn his interests, to understand his way of thinking. None of that mattered. They had an agreement. One that would keep her safe, and she was going to stick to it.

She stopped in front of him. "I was told there was more to the physical act than what you showed me the other day. I have come to see what else there is to know."

She was proud of how steady her voice remained even as she kept her hands pressed together to keep them from trembling.

But a mocking grin tipped one corner of his lips, and she felt the rise of embarrassment start within her. He set his drink down on the desk behind him, and she struggled to keep from turning, taking her cloak, and leaving immediately.

Through the front door if only to shame him.

But wouldn't that ruin her and her family?

Why did this man cause her to lose her senses with such alarming regularity?

"There's a great deal more," he said, crossing his arms over his chest.

She stared at his arms, so casually crossed. She wanted him to touch her. She wanted him to act with the urgency and speed with which he had acted the day of the wedding. She wanted—

Him.

All of him. The uncontrolled Hawk she had never before witnessed. She didn't like this calculating relaxed Hawk she had known for years. This one was the recipient of so much of her ire. She wanted the one who sparked fire within her, who stoked her desire until she thought she would drown in it.

She reached up before she realized what she was about, before she could allow the thought to form in her mind, and she pulled his arms loose, slipping into his embrace before he could stop her. She pressed herself against him, her hands finding their way to his back, to the contours of muscle her fingers seemed to remember.

He smelled faintly of cigar smoke, and she wondered briefly what it was he and Philip did at their club. Perhaps one day he would tell her.

Would she get used to this? Slipping into his home under the cover of darkness to carry out their affair?

The idea had once seemed fanciful and daring, but just then it left her cold and sad. The idea that she would only have this man in snatches suddenly seemed like not enough.

She kissed him, willing the sensations of her body to drown out the noise of her mind, but he didn't kiss her back. Instead he eased her away from him, holding her at arm's length as he captured her gaze.

"Do not try to distract me, pet. I told you not to do anything reckless and yet here you stand. In a bachelor's home. If we are to carry out an affair, I will insist that you do as I say."

She pulled her shoulders out of his grasp. "Is that how this is to be then? I do as you bid?" Fear raced over her skin as she thought of her mother, broken and defeated. "I will not allow such control, Hawk. I already told you as much." She spun about, suddenly wanting her cloak and to flee, but he stopped her, his arms going about her and pinning her to his chest.

He shook his head slightly as he studied her. "You're like a wild animal, pet. Afraid to accept help from anyone you see as a threat."

"Are you a threat?" She hadn't meant to whisper the words, but as she stared up into his dark eyes, she couldn't help but feel the sensation of falling. She curled her fingers into his evening jacket as if to hold on.

"I'm the worst kind of threat," he muttered and kissed her.

WHEN HE HAD FIRST SEEN her there, standing outside the rear door of his townhome, he had thought her a mirage. If he hadn't seen the trail of golden hair escaping the hood of her cloak, he wouldn't have known it was her.

He had told her to wait until he could arrange for them to meet discreetly, but it was obvious she hadn't been able to. The idea that she had sought him out, that she hadn't been able to wait—

Did it mean she was simply spoiled and used to getting what she wished for when she wished for it?

Or did it mean something else?

In the years he had known her, she had never once exhibited the tendencies of the spoiled debutante, and he didn't think her capable of it now.

So, was it just that her desires were too strong to contain? Did she want him that much?

The thought sent warmth flooding through him until chasing closely behind it was the darkness he had evaded his whole life. She had claimed to only want a lover, but such a notion suggested emotion could be kept out of the affair. The very suggestion was ludicrous, especially to him.

Could he keep himself from becoming more to her? Could either of them?

He had brought her to his study, hoping to keep her from the prying eyes of his servants. While he trusted them implicitly, he also didn't trust them to not let something slip to his grandmother. She would demand he marry Caroline immediately if she were to get so much as a whiff of scandal.

And while Caroline had assured him time and again that she had no need for a husband, he couldn't help but let his mind wander. She should have a husband. One to protect her, to see to her happiness, to—

He tore his mouth from hers, the image becoming too real and it left a bitter taste on his tongue.

He didn't want another man to touch her. He wanted her for himself, and that was the one thing he couldn't have.

He had to remember what this was about. She wanted a lover, and he wanted her for as long as he could have her.

Her lips were swollen, her eyelids fluttering as if lost in her own desire. She was so beautiful in the candlelight, and he wanted nothing more than to study her face.

"Hawk." There was a plaintive note in her voice, and he kissed her again before she could open her eyes.

He didn't waste time after that. If he let his mind linger, too many thoughts would crystalize and stop him. And he wanted to take. For once in his life, he wanted to take what was offered him.

He made quick work of the laces at the back of her gown, and the garment slipped from her shoulders. His fingers went to the ties of her corset, tugging at the bow until the entire thing unraveled and he could work his fingers under the ribbons that held it closed. He felt her exhale against his lips as the corset fell away with her chemise.

Only then did he stop, easing her back to hold at arm's length.

She was naked except for her stockings and slippers, and she stood in the pool of her own clothes. The candlelight licked her body with a warm glow, and he tightened at just the sight of her.

"Oh God, you're beautiful." His voice was ragged, and he swallowed, trying to draw a breath, but he was overcome by...her.

But more, she didn't try to hide herself. Her arms remained fluid at her sides, and she let him look, a small, knowing smile on her lips.

She was enjoying this. She was enjoying the way just the sight of her body tortured him. Her round, perfect breasts, the slight swell of her belly, the flare of her hips.

He reached forward to take her hand, to help her step from the ring of her garments, but she pulled her hand away, shaking a finger at him.

"You promised to show me more, and you are wearing far too many clothes to show me anything I haven't yet discovered."

He raised an eyebrow. "We're rather confident for someone who has never done this before."

She tilted her head. "You're wrong in that. I have done this once before. That means I'm no longer an innocent."

Carefully she stepped out of the ring of her clothes, and he watched her, his gaze transfixed as she turned, and—

Sweet Jesus, her bottom. Her perky bottom so round and lush above the lace of her stockings as she walked away from him.

He tore off his jacket and waistcoat, wrenching his cravat so indelicately he nearly choked himself in his struggle to shed his clothes. His boots came next as he leaned against his desk to leverage them off.

The entire time she continued to saunter away from him, her buttocks bouncing as she walked, the lines of her back and shoulders taunting him.

She stopped at the sofa and turned, settling back on it as she considered him. He stilled, one boot still in his hand as she reclined, crossing one leg over the other and leaning back as if she were expecting a show.

The little minx.

She was closer to the fire now, and the light of its flames danced across her, highlighting every valley and crest. He was hard now, painfully so, and he eased his breeches open, shoving them down his legs and stepping free, not caring if he might scare her with his nakedness. She was obviously comfortable, and she had demanded that he show her more.

He pulled his shirt over his head with one hand, and that was it. That was all of him. He studied her, watching her face change as she blatantly took him in, looking her fill of his body. He didn't move. He couldn't move. Watching her study him was the most erotic thing he had ever experienced, and suddenly he forgot what he had planned to do.

He wanted to touch her. All of her. All of the places he hadn't been able to explore the day of the wedding.

Slowly he strode toward her, and her eyes lifted to his, a soft smile unfurling on her lips. But she didn't speak. Instead she opened her arms to him, her legs slipping apart to give him room. He came to her, falling into her arms as he wrapped his own around her, lifting her to his kiss.

Her breasts crushed against his chest, her nipples hard, and he groaned against her mouth, his hands curling into the muscles of her back, tracing the contours of her body.

"Hawk," she murmured against his lips. "Hawk, I feel..."

But he deepened the kiss, his passion overtaking sense, his hands moving furiously across her gorgeous body. He swept his hands down her sides, feeling every curve now instead of the rigid confines of her corset. She arched into him, giving him access to her every part, and he reveled in it.

His erection throbbed, and he shifted, but it only served to nestle it against the softness of her belly. He wrenched his lips from hers.

"Caroline, I don't know how long..."

She opened her eyes, and her fingers stroked back the hair from his forehead. "We have all night," she whispered with a smile.

Time shifted around him, and he pictured this, this moment unfurling a thousand times over for the entirety of a lifetime. He could have a lifetime with Caroline and never grow tired of her. He could never grow tired of this, and he knew he would never be done discovering her, her body, her soul, *her*.

And yet all he had was mere weeks.

Pain gripped him, hot and cutting, and he sucked in a breath and kissed her before he could allow it to gain hold of him. He moved, tracing kisses down her neck, over her collarbones, and finally, *finally* to her succulent breasts.

Her breasts were perfect, small and pert, and he filled his hands with them. She lifted, pushing herself against him, and he pulled one nipple into his mouth, lavishing it with his tongue.

Her fingers spiked through his hair, and she moaned, her legs wrapping around his hips until he was pressed to the hot core of her. He tore his mouth from her breast, his head going back as a moan escaped him, and he couldn't stop himself.

He pressed into her wetness, feeling how ready she was for him.

Not yet. He couldn't. He wanted more of her.

But she moved, lifting her hips into him, a mewling sound slipping from her lips.

It was too much. He gripped her hips and slid into her until he was fully seated against her. The sensation was exquisite, bordering on painful, and he stilled, letting her body adjust to him.

It was a mistake. Her muscles undulated around him, and it was as though she were trying to pull him farther into her. Her tight sheath was more than he could bear, and he bent forward, lapping her other nipple into his mouth as if the taste of her could distract him from the torment she rendered on his body.

But then the minx moved again, lifting her hips against him, moving against him, taking him deeper into her.

"Oh Hawk, that feels so good." Her head was thrown back against the cushions, her eyes shut tight in passion, and he lost his breath at the sight of her.

His hips began to move of their own volition. He withdrew entirely before plunging into her to the hilt. She moaned, her eyes flying open as her hands scrambled for purchase, gripping his arms as he held her.

"Hawk, please." Her voice was rough with passion, and the sound of it sent the last of his control spiraling.

He began to move faster, his hips driving into her, his erection throbbing. Release was so close, but he couldn't. Not yet. He had to give her her pleasure first.

He licked the pad of his thumb and reached between them, flicking the callused finger over her sensitive nub. She reared up, her eyes wide, her head thrown back, a sensual scream slipping from her lips.

"Hawk, I can't. It's—"

He felt her release. She tightened, convulsing around him, and it was all he could do to hold on, to enjoy the feel of her muscles caressing him. She went limp in his arms, and only then did he pull himself from her, lifting her bodily into his arms until he could turn her over, and she was propped on her knees before him, that perky, teasing buttocks perched under his hands.

"Hawk." There was a question in her voice, and he leaned over, sliding his hands along the curve of her back until he whispered in her ear.

"You said you wanted to know everything."

She shivered against him, and his cock twitched against the soft cleft of her buttocks.

He couldn't wait any longer. He reached down and separated her legs, giving him access to her. He slid carelessly into her, heedless of her pleasure, wanting only his. Her buttocks slammed against him, and he knew he wouldn't last long. He kneaded each buttock as he pounded into her, as her cries mounted, as she pushed back against him, taking as much as he gave.

When his release came, it was total and complete, robbing him of breath and strength, and he collapsed, pulling her against him as he spent himself inside of her.

He cradled her, holding her against him as his heart slowed, and his breath returned to normal.

It was only minutes later when he heard her whisper.

"Can we do that again?"

9

S he tried to ignore the sense that something was missing.

The fact of the matter was the thing that was missing was Audrey.

She and Dash had gone to one of his country estates for their wedding trip, and the horrible thing was Caroline didn't know which one. When Audrey had left, Caroline's mind had been slightly muddled with other concerns, and she'd forgotten entirely what Audrey had said.

So, standing on the edge of yet another ball felt quite not the same without her constant companion and friend. She shifted from foot to foot, not entirely sure why she was there in the first place. It was not as though she were on the market for a husband.

As soon as the thought entered her mind, the various places on her person which ached with a newness she still hadn't grown used to sang to remind her just how much she was not on the market.

She had taken a lover.

She'd done it. The very thing that had entered her mind,

the thing that was so scandalous it could ruin her far more than anything Philip had done.

This thought gave her pause.

It was true. Her behavior could end her own societal career as well as put a black mark on her family, and yet she had entered into the bargain far too easily.

Was this what Philip had felt? This unrelenting need to be with another person?

Was that what she felt for Hawk?

She prodded at her feelings, hoping to put into words exactly what it was she felt for him. They had been lovers now for an entire week, and in that time, they had managed to be together four times.

Four.

Her cheeks flamed, and she fanned herself with her empty dance card.

She should have been concerned that it was so easy for her to slip from her home unnoticed and travel to Hawk's townhome, entering through the mews as she had done that first night. He always met her at the door and scuttled her up to his rooms. The entire thing felt sordid and thrilling at the same time, and she wondered when she had allowed herself to grow quite so wanton.

But was it love that drove her? Or lust?

Absently her eyes settled on Philip across the room speaking with Lady Dolores, the debutante whose ball this was. Lady Dolores was the daughter of their mother's friend or card partner or sewing circle companion or some such thing, and Lady Mattingly had promised their attendance to ensure Lady Dolores's night was a success. Otherwise Caroline would have preferred to stay home.

That wasn't entirely true. She would have preferred another night in Hawk's arms.

No one would have noticed her absence at the ball anyway. Philip probably would have been glad for it. But she hadn't stayed home because it was so rare that her mother asked her for anything.

It was rare that her mother asked for *anything* these days.

This would all be far more entertaining if Audrey were there. But would she still stand with Caroline on the periphery of the ball? Or as the Countess of Amberley would she be required to mingle with the other matrons?

Caroline hadn't thought of that. She hadn't thought of how little everyday things would change now that Audrey was married. She had thought of the big ones of course. That was what had sent her into a spiral and into Hawk's arms, but it was the quieter, everyday things she'd forgotten.

She sighed then, her mind not quite up to the task of thinking about such things just then.

"I would think that sigh was meant for me, but I was rather hopeful not to be the subject of your vexation quite so much now."

She started at the sound of Hawk's voice, her eyes darting to his face only to look quickly away.

"What are you doing here?" she hissed.

He was painfully handsome tonight, dressed all in black and his russet hair shaped around his face. He was clean shaven, which she wasn't used to as their encounters usually occurred late in the evening when his beard had grown in during the day.

It was startling to see him so, well...clothed.

"I'm speaking to the sister of a very dear friend of mine." She could feel his gaze on her, but she couldn't meet his eyes. "It will only appear unnatural if you act like it is."

Now she did look at him, aware her cheeks were red with embarrassment.

"I am not acting unnaturally."

He tried to hide a grin. "You are, but if perhaps I speak of something dull and fastidious it will distract you. Have you seen what all this rain has done to the Serpentine? It will be a regular flood soon."

He had adopted such a dry tone, she couldn't stop the snort of laughter that escaped her lips.

Quite quickly she forgot how much she missed Audrey, forgot how awkward it felt to be there without her.

And with this sensation came another of stark dread.

She was getting far too close to Hawk.

Not physically. They couldn't get physically closer than they already had been, but she could feel her emotions turning like the tide based on his nearness. That would never do, and she shifted her gaze, searching out her mother.

"I wasn't aware that you enjoyed debutante balls."

"I don't," he said quickly. "But I enjoy you." He dropped his voice so only she heard the last bit, and she snatched up her dance card to fan herself with it once more.

"You're here to see me?" It took a great deal of strength to keep her voice level.

He had the decency not to look at her as he answered, but she heard the wry note in his voice. "Of course. Why wouldn't I wish to see you?"

He had seen her, all of her, the previous night, when she'd slipped out after her mother had retired for the evening and Philip had gone into his study with a bottle of whiskey and shut the door. He had been doing that a lot as of late, and if she allowed it, her mind would place blame at Lady Winnaretta's feet.

But she was no longer going to allow such fanciful notions to enter her mind. She was determined to take control of her worrying thoughts and make of her life what she wished.

Isn't that what she had done by taking Hawk as her lover?

While she felt a surge of determination, when she looked at him, she felt oddly empty. She had taken what she wanted. She had kept control and gained the thing she wished. So why did her victory feel so hollow?

"I would think a man such as yourself would have plenty of other...better choices." She studied him. "Perhaps another book to read?"

Oddly he looked away from her when he replied, even though his light tone suggested he understood her barb. "I find myself inclined to take in some exercise."

"Exercise? At a ball?"

He looked back at her then, one eyebrow raised. "Isn't this where I would ask you to dance?"

The blood surged to her head and her arms and her toes, her extremities tingling with sudden panic.

"You cannot ask me to dance."

He eyed her. "Why ever not? It's what is done at these things, isn't it?"

"People will talk."

"Talk? You mean they will see me dancing with my best friend's sister when her cousin and constant companion is absent on her wedding trip? Yes, I should think such a thing scandalous."

She didn't miss the sarcasm in his voice, but still, she persisted. "It isn't done."

He blinked. "What isn't done? You're an acquaintance, and I'm asking you to dance. It's exactly what is done."

Her brain scrambled to find another excuse, but just then the orchestra started the first notes of the next dance, and she was without time to come up with something.

"Hawk, I can't."

"If you refuse me now, it will look far more curious than if you simply go along with it."

He was right. The blasted man was right. They had been standing there, heads bent together for far too long, and the only thing that would explain such a coziness was if they paired for the next dance.

Without thinking, she thrust out her arm to take his and stepped into the swirling arrangement of dancers.

"At least it's a quadrille, and you won't be forced to speak to me for the entirety of it."

She knew he had meant it playfully, but suddenly she did wish to speak to him for the whole of it. A waltz would have meant they could have conversed without drawing attention to themselves. Now, in a quadrille, they would hardly have seconds to speak when the dance brought them together at intervals.

But why did she feel such a need to speak to him?

Because they hadn't done much talking in the four nights they had been together, and suddenly she wished to know more of him.

She wanted to know why he had stacks of books littering his rooms. Why was it that he didn't want for a wife? Didn't the title require it? Or was it that he simply didn't wish to marry her?

The thought had bile rising in her throat.

She faltered in her step, and it was only the quick hand of her partner that kept her from falling.

She shouldn't want Hawk to wish for her to be his wife. But that was what he had said that night in the garden. If he were to marry, it would only be her that he would have.

Had he agreed to take her as his lover knowing all along that he would try to make her his wife? Was he planning on seducing her and telling her father so she would be forced to marry him?

Suddenly the dancers were spinning around her in a kaleidoscope of silks and feathers, and her feet could no longer find the floor. The room tilted, and she knew at any moment she would fall.

But then Hawk's arms were around her, spinning her into the final steps of the quadrille, and before she could think properly she was once again standing to the side of the ballroom, her hand properly settled atop Hawk's arm as he led her away from the dancing.

"Are you all right?" he whispered as soon as they were away from the bustle of the guests at the edge of the dancing.

She had thought she had kept her wits about her enough not to show her sudden uneasiness, but of course Hawk would know there was something unusual about her. They were far enough away from the others, but she checked to ensure no one was near enough to hear her.

"Hawk," she started, keeping her voice low. "Did you mean what you said about not wanting a wife?"

A shadow passed over his face, and once more she had the feeling that Hawk had a secret. It would be absurd to think because there was nothing about Hawk that was secretive, but there was most certainly a pain somewhere deep in his past he was hiding.

And why did she wish to suddenly be the one to uncover it? To help him heal?

"I do not want a wife, Caroline. We discuss—"

She cut him off with a wave of her hand at the sternness in his voice.

"I just wished to see if we were still agreed on that point." She watched his face carefully for a reaction, but the shadow only lingered there, his jaw hard.

Yet she couldn't shake the suspicion of her sudden realization. Was Hawk planning to force her hand? Was this how he planned to get her to accept his suit?

Something about it didn't seem right. She had spent far too many years hating this man, and such rage suddenly felt stale.

There was more to Hawk than she had ever guessed, and now she was itching with questions she couldn't ask. This wasn't to be about emotions. Theirs was only a physical relationship.

So why did she want more?

"We should probably separate. It will be enough that we've danced together tonight," she said quickly.

Hawk stepped back and bowed as if he were bidding her good evening. "Are you certain you are all right?"

She nodded, forcing a smile. "Quite. I think I shall get some lemonade and chat with the chaperones for a bit."

He studied her face, and she warmed under the scrutiny. She tried to smile harder, but he only shook his head.

"You're a terrible liar, pet," he muttered and slipped into the crowd.

~

HE WAS GETTING TOO CLOSE.

He had known it the moment his heart constricted at the sight of her standing alone at the edge of the dance floor. He tried to remember if he had ever seen her so alone like that, without Audrey by her side, and he couldn't think of a time when he had.

The enormity of what she must be feeling came to him all at once, and he wanted not to care. He wanted not to understand how deeply her pain must run.

Because he knew what it was like to feel utterly and completely alone.

That was why he had gone to her. That was why he had asked her to dance. If only to relieve her loneliness for just a little while.

But in doing so, had he caused even greater damage?

He had been stupid to think his emotions wouldn't get tangled in their love affair. He was already too much in love with her to have stopped it. And yet he hadn't been able to resist her.

She had dangled the very thing he couldn't have in front of him, and he'd ignored every reason he should have to stay far away from it.

Because he wanted. He wanted all of her forever.

He had only had four nights with her and yet he already knew what he must do.

He must end it.

He wasn't strong enough.

He could have her. Completely and forever, he knew that. She was not the one with the power in the situation due to the simple fact of her sex. One whisper from him and marriage would be the only thing to save her. He felt sick at just the thought and knew he would never do such a thing.

But he could, and that was enough to make him understand what he had to do.

His thirtieth birthday loomed in front of him like the edge of a cliff, and try as he might, there was only blackness before him.

He couldn't take her with him. Whether she chose to marry or not, he couldn't decide her path for her, knowing what he knew.

But he couldn't help but wonder what had come over her at the end of their dance. It was as though she had seen a ghost, and he knew only too well how some thoughts had the power to haunt.

What had she been thinking? Had she remembered him for the scoundrel she thought he was? Or had she suddenly realized what little power she had in their affair?

When Philip stepped in front of him, it was all he could do to keep from exclaiming.

He turned his startled gasp of air into a curse. "Dammit, Philip. Since when have you started sneaking about these things?" As soon as the words left his lips, he regretted them, his eyes moving about the room. "Is she here?" he asked after a beat, his tone more measured.

Philip looked about them as if he were lost, and Hawk realized it wasn't Lady Winnaretta that occupied his thoughts. Which could only mean...

"Is who here?" Philip asked, following Hawk's line of sight. "If you mean my sister, I should think you already know that."

Hawk had never heard Philip raise his voice in all of their friendship, but it reached a note of steel just then that made any rampage look inconsequential.

"Your sister?" Hawk asked, trying for innocence. "I was speaking of Lady Winnaretta."

Philip would not be distracted it seemed, and without comment, he took Hawk's arm, pulling him in the direction of the corridor. Like many townhomes of the *ton*, the walls were adorned with gilt framed portraits of ancestors. This part of the hallway was not illuminated, and the dim light from the other portion of it created leering shadows across the floor from the tilted frames.

Hawk swallowed, remembering his friend knew nothing if only Hawk kept his wits about him.

"You've never danced with my sister before," Philip said without preamble, stopping well out of earshot of any of the other guests.

"Of course I haven't. Your sister despises me."

"And yet you just did."

"Of course I did." He kept his tone level if a little bored, hoping to play the fool. "Did you see how she was standing there?"

Philip raised an eyebrow. "What are you talking about?"

Hawk ran a hand through his hair, releasing an exasperated breath. "Philip, I sometimes worry you go about this world with your eyes half shut." He gestured to the ballroom behind them. "Did it ever occur to you that your sister is without her constant companion for the very first time in her life, and that tonight may well be her first foray into the clutches of society without her?"

Philip blinked, his face losing the tightness of accusation. "Do you mean Audrey?"

"I mean precisely that."

Philip scoffed and waved him off. "Audrey's a wallflower. Caroline only spent time with her so she wouldn't feel so alone at these things."

Hawk couldn't understand his friend's obtuseness at times. But Philip hadn't always been like this. It was only after his broken engagement that he seemed to withdraw behind a curtain of indifference.

It was only Hawk who knew the truth. That Philip was hurting because he had, in fact, truly wished to marry Lady Winnaretta.

If she hadn't lost the baby, his friend very well might have been a different person now.

"Have you no idea what Audrey means to Caroline?"

Philip shrugged. "They're cousins. It's what family means to anyone."

Hawk studied his friend. "You cannot be serious."

"And you cannot think I believe you danced with my sister out of pity."

Hawk laughed. "Who said anything about pity? I was trying to distract her for a bit. She's having to figure out what her life is now. What better way to confuse her than force her to spend time with me?" He grinned as broadly and obnoxiously as he could, and Philip seemed to melt before him, his lips turning up into a grin.

"I suppose you're right. She would have hated that."

Hawk did not like the confidence in his friend's voice, but it had worked to distract him. "Now tell me. Have you seen Lady Winnaretta?"

Philip's gaze moved over Hawk's shoulder in the direction of the ballroom, but his eyes remained unfocused. It was as though he had searched every ballroom for five years hoping to see a sign of her only to be disappointed, and now, even when prompted, Philip couldn't gather the enthusiasm to put forth for the task.

"Lady Winnaretta isn't here." His tone was no longer indifferent. It was almost dangerous.

Hawk stilled, taking in the rest of his friend he had missed earlier as he had been overwhelmed with his concern for Caroline.

Philip's cravat sat slightly askew, and his waistcoat didn't quite match his jacket as though he had dressed in a hurry. It looked like he hadn't tended to his toilette in days, and dark shadows lingered under his eyes.

Hawk sucked in a breath. "You've seen her."

Philip slid him a glance. "All of London has seen her."

He made to move around Hawk then, almost as if he planned to brush him off, but Hawk stopped him with a hand to his shoulder.

"No, Philip. You've seen her. You've talked to her."

When had that happened? When had his best friend confronted the ghost of his past? Where had Hawk been if not there to comfort his friend?

He had been between the legs of the same friend's little sister.

Hawk swallowed, suddenly feeling a thousand times the scoundrel Caroline purported him to be.

"When?" He tried for calm, but his voice skittered on the word. "When did you see her, Philip?"

Philip tried again to get around him, and again Hawk stopped him with a hand.

Philip wouldn't meet his eye as he said, "Four days ago."

Four days ago Hawk had been buried in his affair with Caroline. He couldn't have said if the sky was still blue by then let alone what his best friend had done.

"Christ, man, what happened? *How* did it happen?"

Philip met his gaze now. "It went about how you would think it would. She didn't wish to see me."

"How did you convince her to?"

Philip scrubbed a hand over his face. "I didn't," he muttered between his teeth. "She sent her bloody maid to deal with me."

Hawk leaned back, unable to stop the grimace. "Mathilda."

Philip made a noise somewhere between being sick and hoping to die.

Mathilda was descended from a long line of Lowe

servants, and her stature and resilience were formidable. Hawk had been on the receiving end of one of her scoldings more than once when Lady Winnaretta was still an active part of their circle of friends, and he didn't regret the lack of contact he had with the woman now for that reason.

"She hasn't changed. I'll give her that much," Philip whispered, swallowing hard.

"Did she say why Lady Winnaretta wouldn't see you?"

"No." Philip spoke the word succinctly and dryly, his shoulders falling. "I think perhaps I am expected to think of a hundred reasons why she wouldn't wish to see me, but I had thought we might—" His words stumbled, and he coughed, his eyes closing as if in pain.

Hawk touched his shoulder once more, softly this time and reassuringly. "It's all right, mate. I know. I thought she would have seen you as well. So much time has passed. Surely she must feel differently about what happened."

Philip's gaze was hot when he opened his eyes. "Feel differently? About losing her child? About losing William's child?"

There was fury and hurt in Philip's voice, but it wasn't directed at Hawk. It was directed at himself.

"You must stop blaming yourself for what happened." The words, Hawk knew, were useless. They were the same words spoken to him by more than one concerned family member, by his grandmother more times than he could remember.

"Then who is there to blame?" Philip's tone was like a man dying, and it was the first time in years Hawk had witnessed his friend's pain rather than his manufactured indifference.

It cut Hawk deeply, and he wished not for the first time

to take away his friend's pain, to carry the burden himself as he already carried his own.

Once Philip had been the light of their circle of friends. He was always quick with a joke and the first to make someone smile on a low day.

But not anymore.

That hadn't happened in quite some time in fact, and it was a wonder to Hawk that Philip managed to get through each day.

For a moment Hawk remember those years before the war. When for a small space in time he had been happy too. But he knew the truth of happiness. It was always fleeting and more than anything, he didn't deserve it.

"Sometimes there's no one to blame," he said now, and he wondered which of them he was speaking to. "Sometimes these things just happen, and we're forced to put our life together differently than it was before if only to move on."

Philip swallowed, his lips a tense line. "But what if I don't want to move on?"

Hawk closed his eyes and gathered himself. He opened them and said, "It looks as though Lady Winnaretta already has though, mate."

He didn't wish to be the one who said it. He didn't wish to be the one to have to tell his friend to let go of the woman he had loved for years. But in the end, Hawk was his friend. And true friends sometimes did difficult things.

This was one of them.

"Do you know what would be good right now? A stiff drink and a warm fire. Come along, mate."

Philip went without resistance, and Hawk wondered why he regretted that he was taking Philip home instead of Caroline.

10

So, this is what it was like. Having a lover.

They had fallen into a routine that once might have frightened her but now seemed utterly normal and even ordinary.

It was far too easy for her to slip from her home. Her father was often out at his club or heaven knew where else. Philip. Poor Philip. She hadn't seen much of him since discovering Lady Winnaretta had returned to society, and she wondered if that were deliberate on his part. There was a small worry somewhere deep inside of her for her brother, but it seemed so faint now.

Now that her life was consumed by Hawk.

Did she care less for her brother? No, it wasn't that at all. But rather her outlook had changed on what had transpired between Philip and Lady Winnaretta all those years ago, and instead of the memory inciting immediate anger, it only caused her reflection.

The truth was she didn't know what had happened with Lady Winnaretta, but what she believed to have happened had lost its menacing edge.

As she lay with her head in Hawk's lap, his deep, even voice reading to her, the fire snapping in the hearth, she traced the arm he had absently placed across her chest, and she tried to examine her own feelings.

But all she felt was languid. She was liquid, empty, and bare as though Hawk had taken away all the worry that festered within her. He had taken away everything. The tension, the brooding, the tendency to panic. In its place, she was left with...space. There was suddenly space within her own mind to reflect, and likely for the first time in her life, she was able to hear her own thoughts instead of having them race past her.

She felt...free.

She hadn't considered this when she thought of the relations between a man and a woman. She had only been witness to the terrible things someone could do to another. She had never considered the good things that might come of it.

So it was that she lay there in wonder. Wondering at how her mind could be so still. At how she could absorb the story Hawk read aloud to her.

Her spiraling thoughts from the ball seemed so absurd now. Hawk would never reveal their secret. She knew that, and yet she couldn't fathom why the idea had caused her such panic that night.

She looked up at him, the firelight wavering over his chiseled features, casting shadows but sparking light all at once. It was so very much like the man himself that she couldn't stop her heart from clenching. There was so much more to Hawk than she had let herself see.

Watching him in the firelight she was suddenly struck with the realization that she knew very little about him and yet she knew everything about him. He had been a part of her life for so long she didn't think anyone could be more familiar to her, but then she couldn't have said a single real thing about him.

She was seized by a sudden sense of lacking, as though she couldn't be as close as she wished to be with Hawk if she didn't immediately know everything about him. She blinked, feeling the totality of such a thought, and wondering where it had come from. This wasn't at all what she had wished for, but then she heard herself speaking.

"Hawk," she began, tentatively interrupting the steady cadence of his voice. "What was it like? Growing up at Stonegate Manor with your grandmother."

He glanced at her as he turned a page. "Lady Caroline, whatever are you speaking of? Are you truly exhibiting an interest in my childhood?"

The barb was well deserved as she had never before bothered to allow him to speak. She closed her eyes, ashamed, and swallowed her pride.

"I may have been too quick to assume things concerning your person, Lord Stonegate. I wish to give you the opportunity to explain yourself."

He laughed and closed the book, setting it aside as he pulled her more snugly against him.

"Well, I suppose there isn't much to my childhood. I think it was fairly typical of any young boy in the aristocracy."

She wrinkled her nose. "I hardly think that at all. I've met your grandmother, remember?"

Something warm came into his eyes then at the mention of his grandmother. "She is a rather formidable woman, isn't she?"

"Formidable and kind and considerate. You're incredibly fortunate to have her, you know."

He propped an elbow on the arm of the sofa and leaned his head on his fist as if settling into his remembrances.

"She is at that, and I do know how lucky I am. I only wish I could have done more for her earlier in my life."

She moved her head, her hair crackling against his lap as she tried to get a better look at him. "Do more for her? I would say you've done quite a bit. You're a good grandson, Hawk."

He raised one eyebrow in suspicion. "You're rather free with the compliments this evening. Why the sudden interest in my past?"

She pushed away his arm and sat up, turning so she could face him. "It just occurred to me how much of you I've based on my own prejudices. I don't think I can say as I know what's really you and what I've fabricated about you," she said, tucking her legs up and putting her chin on her knees.

He laughed. "Well then. What is it you'd like to know?"

"What was your childhood like? Was it terribly lonely?"

A line appeared between his brows. "Lonely? Why would you say that?"

She shrugged. "I've always had Philip and Audrey and Gavin and even sour Ethan. There was always someone coming through the house with whom I could play. But it's as though you had no one."

Wrinkles appeared at the corners of his eyes as he smiled softly. "I didn't have no one though. I had Philip, and more importantly I had my grandmother. She was a young grandmother, you see, and still up to quite a bit of sport when I was a child."

Caroline picked up her head. "Lady Sherrill?" She tried to picture the small, cheery woman as being anything related to sporty.

Hawk nodded earnestly. "Oh yes. She taught me to ride herself. She wouldn't leave it to tutors. She feared they would not teach me properly. And she was damn talented at fishing."

She couldn't stop her eyebrows from going up. "Lady Sherrill fished?"

"Still does. It's hard to keep her away from the ponds. I have a terrible time reminding her to look after her health and not catch a chill."

Suddenly an image of dainty Lady Sherrill fishing at the trout pond in the gardens of Stonegate Manor flashed into her mind, and with it, the idea that Caroline would love to see it one day. Her heart thudded in her chest, and she licked her suddenly dry lips. She shouldn't be having such thoughts. That was simply not how their relationship was going to end, and it wouldn't do to indulge in such fanciful notions.

"She must have missed your grandfather. And her son," she added, realizing suddenly the enormity of what Lady Sherrill, and Hawk, had lost.

Some of the light went out of Hawk's face then, and she regretted having said anything, but then he seemed to rally, his face showing a kind of sad joy.

"I think she missed the man she had married. My grandfather tried very hard to forget himself after my father died. I can't imagine how painful it is to lose your own son."

"You lost your father," she said, her voice almost a whisper.

She had no fond feelings toward her own father, but the vacant look in Hawk's eyes made her wonder what kind of bond he had with the father he had lost.

He made a noise then that might have been a laugh, but it was hollow and forlorn. "I think I was rather spared the worst of it. I was only a little more than three when my parents died, and while I have a few snatches of memory of them, the picture I have of my parents is largely composed of the snippets Grandmother has told me about them."

"You were only three?" She hadn't known he was so young when he had lost them, and she felt a stab of longing.

Longing for the time when her mother had been whole and would play games with them, helping Caroline to dress as a princess and Philip as the knight-errant. She had always hated that game and demanded her mother allow her to slay the dragons and not Philip because Philip was afraid of his own shadow.

Hawk had never had even a chance to form such memories, and she was grateful all at once that he had Lady Sherrill.

He nodded, but his eyes had taken on a faraway look as though he were seeing another time. Did he often try to recall his own memories of his parents? Was it something that haunted him? Or did it serve as a constant companion, a reminder of the preciousness of time?

She shifted along the sofa and came against the crook of his arm, nestling herself into his embrace as he absently wrapped his arm around her.

She wanted to ask more. She wanted to know how his parents had died, but the vacant look on his face prevented her from speaking. She didn't wish to mistakenly tread on sensitive wounds.

"Did you know I've been thinking about what you said?" She wrapped an arm around him, drawing him closer against her.

Her question seemed to pull him back from whatever dark place he had wandered. "What is that?"

"I've been thinking about what you said."

He laughed softly. "Dear God, that can't be good, can it?"

She leaned back so she could look at him, reaching up a single finger to feel the roughness of his beard. "You asked me if I ever had a single good thought about you, remember?"

He closed his eyes as if in pain, but he was clearly trying to hide a smile at the same time. "I did ask that of you, didn't I? How foolish of me."

"It wasn't foolish at all. I had judged you unfairly, and your question forced me to think otherwise."

He tilted his head, taking her in, and she felt the heat of his gaze. She suddenly worried her one good thought wasn't enough, and she spoke before she allowed her insecurities to get the better of her.

"I was thinking Philip was lucky to have you." She said the words so quickly she was worried Hawk might not have understood them when his gaze narrowed in question. She fingered the folds of his shirt, unable to look at him as she went on. "I was thinking how hard it must be to leave home and go to school. I remember watching Philip ride away in the carriage, and I was so sad because there wouldn't be anyone at school who knew our games, and I wondered who he would have to play with. But then he came home on the first holiday stammering on about this boy he had met, but I didn't understand because he kept talking about hawks. It was all very confusing for me at the time, but he was happy, and that's really all that mattered to me."

He watched her for several seconds after she finished, and she wanted to look away under such scrutiny, but she couldn't tear her eyes from him. She tried a soft smile, but really her heart ached for the little boy who had lost his parents so young and had grown up with only his grandmother as a companion.

But maybe that wasn't quite true. Speaking of the memory of Philip had jarred loose several other memories of Hawk spending holidays with them when they were all much older. Another thought, a more confusing thought, suddenly tripped over the rest and clouded them out.

She touched his chin again. "Hawk, what happened when your grandmother remarried?"

HE WASN'T sure what had sparked this journey into their childhood memories, but he had never before captured her attention the way he did now. That was unless his mouth was on a part of her body the rest of the world never saw.

But it was as though something had spurred her on, and he wondered if it had to do with the return of Lady Winnaretta.

"When Grandmother remarried, Stonegate Manor was suddenly very empty. I didn't blame her, of course. She had found happiness again when I never thought she could. It was a blessing really." He stopped, and it was as if he were looking back through time and reliving that moment in his life again. "It's the quiet really that I remember. I came back on holiday that first time after her wedding, and I just couldn't understand why it was so quiet. The silence was unnerving."

She stirred in his arms. "That's when you showed up at our doorstep so unexpectedly." She cupped his cheek in her hands, her eyes pools of concern. "I thought you were just there to take Philip away from me, but it wasn't that at all. I'm so sorry, Hawk."

He could hear the real sorrow in her voice, but he smiled, trying to banish it.

"You were only a child. You couldn't have known why I was there."

She frowned. "I could have at least been more open-minded about it."

"You were rather a grump then."

She playfully smacked his chest, but she laughed while she did it.

His mind continued to wind through the memory, and he sobered, recalling just how Caroline had been at that age.

She had been grumpy, but she had also been guarded, and he supposed it was then she had become so protective of Philip.

"Pet," he started after she had settled once more in his arms. "I wonder if you'll tell me something."

He thought his heart never beat so furiously as it did then, and he prepared for the real possibility she would close up on him.

"What is it?" Her voice was suspicious but not brusque.

"Your mother. You mentioned there was a time when she would play games with you and Philip, but she seems so remote now. So distant. Did something happen to her?"

He had expected her to withdraw mentally from him, but instead she stood, slipping from his arms. His hands trailed after her as she moved away from the sofa, wandering as though aimlessly through the stacks of books set upon the floor. She touched the tops of them as she passed as though marking her way so she could find her way back. He watched her, unable to speak as he studied the way she moved about the room.

She stopped at his desk and leaned into it, her palms flat against the wood, and still he waited.

He had never seen her like this. Caroline had always been a whirlwind, rushing through his life in a spout of insults and accusations. This Caroline was quiet, contemplative, and reflective.

He wasn't sure how long they stayed like that, her at his desk and him waiting, but finally she broke the silence by straightening, turning back to him.

"My father's infidelities came as a shock to my mother. I think it destroyed the foundation on which she built her life." She spoke the words coldly as though she were removed entirely from the affair.

He stood slowly, easing his way up from the sofa as though he were trying not to spook a wounded animal.

"Your father's infidelities?" He knew it was quite common for men to stray from their societal marriages, especially arranged ones. Women did the same, in fact, and so Caroline's statement left him wondering. Did her mother believe hers a love match? Was this what Caroline had witnessed that had confused her about love?

Her chin was firm as she said, "My father had taken a lover, and my mother discovered it. I'm not sure," she said, a wrinkle coming to her brow. "I was still quite young then, and I wasn't entirely sure what was happening at the time. I only pieced together the whole of it later when I heard the upstairs maids gossiping."

Hawk pictured a young, impressionable Caroline, listening at doors to more worldly servants whispering about their employers. He knew all too well how quickly her mind deviated to the worst possible scenario, and his stomach clenched in anticipation of what she might say next.

"What did the maids say?" he asked after a time.

She moved, sliding her hands along the carving that marked the edge of the desk. "They said my father had taken an opera singer as a lover, and he had set her up with apartments in Bloomsbury." She laughed, the sound dry. "I wonder how much that had cost. It rather makes sense now though why Father was suddenly absent so often." She stopped when she reached the corner of the desk, her fingers trailing the scrollwork there. "He had a routine, and I learned to plan my lessons by it so I may see him when he returned in the evenings. But one day he didn't come home." Her voice became soft, wistful, and he knew she had fallen into her own memory. "He used to bring me things sometimes. Little trinkets he had picked up from a stall in Covent Garden or a fresh spray of flowers from a cart he had passed on his way home." Her fingers paused in their exploration, and her voice hardened. "But then he stopped coming home, and my mother began hiding in her rooms." She looked up, her eyes wide as though remembering he was there for the first time. "I think it was then that you began coming on holidays more often."

He had been so absorbed in watching her it took him a moment to realize she addressed him. "Yes, it was." He had to clear his throat from the sudden tightness.

All too quickly the picture of Caroline filled in. She had been witness to the destruction of her parents' marriage while Philip had not. Philip had been spared the turmoil by virtue of being born a son and thus destined for schooling while Caroline had been forced to remain at home.

His chest squeezed, for him and for her, two lost young people on the verge of their lives, already scarred by the lives of their parents.

Something shifted inside of him then, and it was as though the blackness moved, morphing into something else like it was reaching for a memory, something just out of reach. But as quickly as it happened, the blackness returned, closing in on his earliest memories, and he was left with the same void he had always faced.

Caroline was studying him, and he blinked to bring her back into focus.

"Do you know what I think? I think that's enough melancholy for one evening. Don't you agree?"

Her eyes narrowed at his question, and her lips parted as though she wished to say something, but then she seemed to change her mind. She smiled instead and said, "I do believe you're right. The hour grows late, doesn't it?" She feigned a yawn that was ruined by a laugh. "And you are keeping me from my bed." Her expression turned seductive, and his body tightened at the sight of it.

How she had the power to turn about his emotions like that was beyond him, but it was something he planned to enjoy while the time remained. He led her through the connecting door to his rooms. He worried how easy it was, how familiar. He had been right about them learning each other's bodies. In the few weeks of their affair, they had fallen into a routine, and now it was nothing to help each other undress, to lead her to the bed and lay her down upon it.

When they made love that night, it was with a quiet desperation as if they both understood the other had scars they had not fathomed. It was as though they could heal each other through their touch, through their kisses, through the very connection of their bodies. And when they finished, they slept soundly like they hadn't before in the other nights they had stolen together.

But all too soon the first light of dawn was brushing the sky, and he was forced to nudge her awake, a careful prodding along her spine as she lay draped across him.

"Mmm," she mumbled. "Not yet."

He kissed the top of her head. "You say that every morning, and every morning I fall victim to your wishes and you stay yet a little longer." He stroked her hair, letting the tresses fall through his fingers. "You were such a cautious mouse when I first met you, and I fear my rakish ways have corrupted you."

She sat up at this, enough to prop her head on her arms splayed across his chest. "Does this mean I'm right? You are a terrible influence?"

He couldn't help but smile at the hopeful expression on her features. "You are absolutely right, pet."

She laughed and surged forward to capture him in a distracting kiss. He wrenched himself free, easing her away. "As corrupting as I am, you are entirely far more dangerous." He slipped from the bed and picked up his dressing gown, shrugging into it. "Dress," he instructed. "And do not try to convince me to let you stay a moment longer."

He left the room before her pouting expression and tousled hair could make him forget his senses.

She emerged from the bedchamber moments later, her gown horribly wrinkled and her hair in a plain braid along her shoulder. He hated these moments the most. Watching her leave. He flexed his hands to keep from grabbing her the way he wished. He wanted her forever, and that was the very thing he didn't have.

He remembered then what she had told him last night, and he wondered if she would ever recover from her wounds. He sincerely hoped so. She deserved happiness, a partner to help her through life. But again, as soon as he thought it, he dismissed it. He could never stand the idea of her belonging to someone else.

But then he wouldn't be there to be plagued by such a notion, would he?

He kissed her, softly, trying to keep his body from touching hers, from igniting the fire that always seemed ready at her nearness.

She was nearly to the door when she turned back. "I was thinking. Your birthday is only a couple of weeks away. Perhaps we should do something to celebrate."

Dread fell like a brick to the bottom of his stomach as his entire body clenched as if preparing for an attack. "My birthday?"

She turned, her fingers busy at the tie of her cloak, and she seemed so young then, so innocent.

She nodded. "Your birthday. It's the twenty-sixth of July. I haven't forgotten." She laughed, the smile traveling all the way to her eyes. "It's hard to forget when it's one of my most cherished memories."

He scrambled, trying to recall why his birthday would be a part of her favorite memories when really he tried to avoid the thing every year.

Her face softened. "You don't remember? It was after you returned from your grand tours, and Philip got the idea to make you a birthday cake." She laughed, more heartily now, and suddenly he remembered.

"He set me on fire with the candles." He frowned. "I can see why that is such a fond memory for you."

Her expression turned pensive. "If only he had been successful. That footman was far too quick with the pitcher of water."

He shook his head. "It's so hard getting good help, isn't it?"

She leaned forward and touched her lips to his. "I promise I shan't try to make you a birthday cake." She trailed her fingers down the front of his dressing gown, her hand dipping lower until he was forced to catch her wrist.

She looked him in the eye as she said, "But I can't promise I won't set you on fire."

She left him then, in a mess of his own emotions. While his body hummed with desire at her words, his chest filled with the pain of reality.

She could promise anything, but by the time his birthday arrived, he would be gone.

11

W hen Audrey appeared at the breakfast table the following week, Caroline thought she was seeing a specter.

With a jolt, she realized she'd lost track of the days.

Honestly, it was rather easy.

Her days were filled with tending to whatever social obligation for which her mother had promised her attendance. If there were any, that was. But her nights. Well, her nights were all her own.

She would slip off through the basements, the servants hardly taking notice now. After all, it wasn't as though her parents were concerned. Why should the servants be?

Caroline was far older than the usual, naive debutante. Perhaps they thought her capable. Perhaps they simply didn't care.

Her brother had taken to going out most nights now. Presumably to his club, but Hawk had never been sure.

He had been taciturn when it came to the subject of her brother since that night at the debutante ball when he'd asked her to dance. Whenever she had brought up the subject of Philip or Lady Winnaretta, he had quickly changed the subject.

She hadn't thought anything of it really. After all, Philip and Lady Winnaretta was a subject of some contention between them. It would be natural for him to avoid it, but now that Philip had developed an odd pattern of disappearing, she couldn't help but worry.

But then she'd developed her own pattern of disappearing.

She wondered suddenly if Philip had taken a lover. Was it Lady Winnaretta? Had he resumed the dangerous relationship that had gotten him into trouble the first time? How could he be so stupid?

It wasn't until she thought of her brother being in danger that she realized she had taken the same course of action. It had given her pause but only momentarily. She didn't have the possible future that Philip did, so it mattered little what might happen to her and Hawk.

But every night it was growing more difficult to leave Hawk, and it worried her. She stayed later, sometimes until dawn began to light the sky, and she risked being discovered by her father who always went for a ride in the park at first light. She had narrowly missed him a time or two.

Even though she was aware of the danger, it didn't help her to be more cautious. She still toyed with the edge of discovery as though it meant nothing to her. But really it was because Hawk meant more.

She wasn't sure when it happened, but the physical relationship she had hoped to keep firmly in her grasp had turned into something else entirely. Had she known it were possible, she would have guarded herself against it. But she hadn't been prepared for the comfortable familiarity that had fallen over them in a few short weeks.

When she had first started slipping into Hawk's home, it was all they could do to make it back to his rooms before making love. But now it had settled into something else.

They lingered over a late supper sometimes. He was teaching her about whiskey and sonnets and even, God forfend, Shakespeare's plays. She had never been one to read before, her mind too agitated to settle to a story, but when Hawk read to her, it was the only time the whirling thoughts in her head quieted enough for contemplation.

Well, not the only time.

But the other times were not meant for anything quiet.

He had taught her things about her own body of which she never would have dreamed. He did things to her, showed her things, discovered things she hadn't thought possible.

It should have been alarming, the depth and complexity their simple love affair had attained, but when she thought of Hawk, she couldn't bring herself to worry.

At some point, she had come to trust him implicitly since that day she had lain with her head in his lap as she asked him about his childhood.

She eyed her breakfast now, but her stomach heaved in response. She set a hand to it, willing the queasiness to subside. She'd often been unwell in the mornings lately, and she believed her late nights were having a disastrous effect on her.

She yawned just as Audrey came through the breakfast room door, and she froze, her hand indelicately covering her gaping mouth.

Audrey's smile was devilish. "Not sleeping well, cousin? Whatever could be keeping you up?"

Caroline jolted, upsetting the flatware on the table as she stood. "Audrey. What are you doing here?"

Audrey's smile turned mocking. "What am I doing here? Am I no longer welcome now that I'm married?"

Caroline shook her head swiftly. "It isn't that. It's just that you weren't expected."

Audrey's face fell. "I must announce myself now?"

Caroline shook her head again, burying her face in her hands. "No, that's not what I meant at all. Oh Audrey, I'm terribly tired, and this is such a surprise." She moved around the table to take her cousin into her embrace. "Welcome home!" she said, feeling the words deeply as Audrey's arms wrapped around her.

They had only been separated a little more than two weeks, but it was enough to feel the chasm that was likely to grow between them as Audrey's new life as a wife and possibly a mother took her attention away from other matters.

Caroline understood, and she would cherish what little time she had with her cousin. After all, it wasn't as though Audrey was all she had any longer.

The thought had her stiffening in Audrey's arms, and her cousin eased her away, her expression curious.

"Whatever is the matter with you, Caroline? Has my absence truly caused you such distress?" Audrey's tone was playful as if her being away couldn't possibly have upset Caroline so, but the fact of the matter was it had.

"Yes." Caroline shook her cousin the slightest bit. "You know very well it would." She looped her arm through Audrey's and pulled her in the direction of the breakfast table. "Now sit and tell me all about your trip."

Audrey laughed and waved off Caroline's attempt to mother her. "It was a wedding trip to the countryside. It's about as exciting as you might imagine. I want to know what happened here while I was away." Her tone was suggestive, and Caroline knew all too well what she implied.

She chose another tact. "I would think your wedding trip would be the most exciting moment of your life so far. Surely you saw interesting things."

Audrey's face flushed, and she avoided Caroline's gaze. "We didn't see much really. Bad weather and such, you know."

"Oh." Caroline couldn't stop the grin as Audrey continued to avoid her gaze.

She knew perfectly well what her cousin's cryptic avoidance meant, but Audrey didn't know she knew. For all Audrey understood, she was the same Caroline she had left behind. The adamant, stubborn, determined headstrong woman well on her way to being a spinster.

Caroline hadn't thought of this. She had only thought of how her affair with Hawk would affect her. She hadn't thought how it might change things between her and the rest of the world. The world shifted beneath her feet again, and she reached out, gripping the table as if to stop everything from changing around her.

She closed her eyes against it, willing the sensation that she was falling to stop, but knowing that it wouldn't.

She opened her eyes and turned to her cousin.

"I need to tell you something," she said and stood, bringing her cousin with her without waiting for a reply.

This was ridiculous. She was a grown woman with desires and wants, and she was done hiding them from those she cared about when quite frankly it didn't matter. None of it mattered.

Because she and Audrey would always be close no matter how their lives tried to separate them, and Caroline was done letting the world make her feel as though she were losing control. She was done with all of it.

"Caroline, what are you—"

Caroline dragged them out onto the terrace and into the summer sunshine, but she didn't stop. She didn't stop until she reached her folly, the very one where she first had the idea of taking Hawk as a lover. That night seemed so long ago now, and yet the memory was still so fresh to her.

She closed the door behind them, and only then did she face Audrey.

"Hawk and I are having an affair," she said without preamble.

She wasn't sure what reaction she expected, but it was likely not the one she got.

Audrey's lips spread into a bountiful smile, and she exclaimed, "Well, that's just splendid! How did it happen?"

Her cousin's eyes were wide and curious. Caroline hadn't seen someone so eager since her father was training a new hunting spaniel.

"Audrey," Caroline said, stepping forward. "I just told you I've been ruined. That I'm mired in scandal with a known rake."

Audrey wrinkled her nose. "I don't think Hawk is a rake. I'm fairly certain you fabricated that bit."

Caroline knew Audrey was right, and she wondered when she realized she had painted a blacker picture of Hawk than he deserved.

Was it when he had saved her from drowning? Or when she had learned of his charity in his parish? Or perhaps it went further than that. Back to the house party that had started all of this, and she'd been able to witness how Hawk had cared for his grandmother.

Caroline shook her head, attempting to dislodge the

distracting thoughts. "That doesn't matter. The fact is I'm ruined."

Audrey shrugged. "You're only ruined if someone discovers it. Have you been discreet?"

"Of course we have."

Audrey shrugged again. "Then what is there to worry over? Come." She moved to the side of the folly and dropped to the floor in the sea of cushions propped against the wall. "Tell me all about how it happened. Was it terribly romantic?"

It was Caroline's turn to wrinkle her nose. "Since when have you been one to sully yourself with romantic flights of fancy?" She dropped to the cushions beside her cousin. "Is this what marriage has done to you?"

Audrey's smile never dimmed. "I believe so. Isn't it grand?"

"Grand?" Caroline shook her head. "It's even affected your vocabulary."

Audrey laughed and swatted her hand playfully. "Now tell me about Hawk. What's happened?"

Caroline opened her mouth to do so but quickly closed it, realizing she wasn't sure where to begin. She chewed her lower lip before saying, "I'm afraid it all started at your wedding breakfast." She was flooded with shame as soon as the words spilled from her lips, but Audrey's quick laugh had her puzzled.

"I was right. I can't wait to tell Dash."

Caroline's stomach flipped. "Tell Dash? You can't tell Dash anything. What are you talking about?"

Audrey's expression dimmed. "I tell Dash everything. And besides, he already suspected that's what happened at the wedding breakfast."

"Already suspected it? But how? We were..." She had

meant to say they were so careful, but honestly she couldn't remember much about that day before she found herself locked in her rooms with Hawk.

Audrey patted her arm. "I'm sure no one noticed who wasn't looking for it, but Dash and I had had our suspicions since the house party." Her cousin's eyes took on a faraway look then. "I suppose that house party was responsible for many things. How odd." Her eyes regained their focus as she said, "Do you recall how Philip received the invitation to the house party?"

Caroline shrugged. "Hawk is his best friend. I always thought it came naturally. Why?"

Audrey waved it away. "It's nothing. I'm sure of it. So, what is to happen with this grand love affair the two of you have embarked on?"

"Nothing." She said the word quickly, but even she could hear the defensive note to it. "I mean it's exactly as we wish it to be. I have no desire to take a husband, and Hawk does not wish for a wife."

Through the whole of the explanation, Caroline had watched Audrey's face fold. "Are you certain that's what the two of you want?"

Caroline nodded. "Of course." Only she no longer felt any kind of certainty in her own worlds.

She thought of those nights when they lingered before retiring to bed. She had learned so much of Hawk's childhood, of the games he and Philip would play when they were at Stonegate Manor on school holidays, of how clearly he remembered the first time they had met. It pained her to think she didn't remember their first meeting. She likely had been too young at the time, but now she wished she could remember it.

She knew Hawk more deeply now than she had known

anyone in all of her life, even Audrey, and while she wanted to insist on the terms of the affair, she felt a newly budding sense of doubt.

It was as though Audrey sensed her weakness and asked, "Have you asked Hawk why he doesn't want for a wife?"

Caroline remembered that time right here in the folly when Hawk had told her he'd only marry her if he ever married at all, and she remembered his reluctance in speaking of his parents' deaths.

She shook her head. "I think Hawk is carrying scars similar to mine, I'm afraid." She toyed with the folds of her gown before continuing. "Audrey, are you happy with Dash?" Caroline knew the answer to this question. It was obvious in Audrey's every move now. The way she laughed so easily. The way she always seemed to be smiling. The way Dash looked at her...

Hadn't Hawk pointed that out?

Audrey's face sobered, and she leaned forward. "I think the question you mean to ask is whether or not all men are like your father. Is that what you're trying to find out?"

Caroline sucked in a breath. She wanted to refute it, but the look on Audrey's face stopped her.

"You're forgetting that my own father is not a paragon of moral virtue," she said.

Caroline stilled. Audrey was right. Caroline had forgotten. Audrey's father was likely worse than her own. He was so terrible, in fact, they rarely spoke of him. That was probably why she had forgotten.

She gripped Audrey's hands. "Oh lud, Audrey, what is the matter with me? I had forgotten, and I'm sorry. I shouldn't—"

Audrey shushed her and squeezed her hands. "This isn't

about my father. It's about yours. Are you going to let his behavior determine your future?"

Caroline licked her lips. "But what if Hawk turns out to be just like him?"

Audrey frowned. "I think you've already discovered for yourself that he's not."

While she knew Audrey's words to be true, there was still a lingering sense of doubt she couldn't quite shake.

Perhaps it was the change of season around them as they moved deeper into summer, and she realized just how long they'd been carrying on their affair. Or perhaps it was Hawk's birthday, only a week away now, and the ritual of it suggested something permanent. She regretted having brought it up, but she had been caught up in the domesticity of the moment, and she'd been struck with the idea of doing something nice for Hawk.

"Audrey, have you ever made a cake?" she asked, trying as hard as she could to ignore the alarm bells ringing in her head.

HE HADN'T BEEN PAYING attention.

He had let things go too far, and his time was up.

He wasn't sure when it had happened or how, but suddenly his thirtieth birthday was only three days away. He had to end it. Tonight.

The thought robbed him of breath, and he bent over his desk, clutching his stomach as though it were real pain that threaded through him.

He couldn't let it go on. He couldn't leave her to linger when he left for Stonegate Manor, wondering if he would ever return. Because in his mind, he couldn't see himself coming back. He couldn't see anything. And that left him no choice.

He had to end it with her. He had to give her the freedom to go on without him.

Because the thought of her spending the rest of her life alone was worse than the thought of her with another man.

At least that was what he told himself.

But when he thought of her with another, it made him sick, and he couldn't let such an idea surface.

He waited for her in the mews as he had taken to doing, the night air biting, the darkness complete around him. There was no moon tonight, and he felt it somehow fitting as the blackness closed in on him. Only the light from the lamps by the door gave any illumination to the yard.

He didn't like the fact that she was forced to cover the short part of the alley between the main road and the mews by herself, but it was the only way to ensure their affair remained a secret. Anyone could have seen him escorting her along the alley, but if she trekked it alone and slipped into the shadows before disappearing, their secret remained safer if not entirely undiscoverable.

He heard her footsteps long before she rounded the corner and opened the back gate. He was ready for her, his arm outstretched, and she took his hand silently just as she did every night.

Together, they slipped through the back door and up to his rooms. His townhome was large, and his grandmother never frequented it. He'd taken over the countess's sitting room adjacent to his own bedchamber for his books, and it was here he took her every night. He never took her directly to his bedchamber. The act would have cheapened what it was between them, and he wouldn't make a harlot out of her. Even if she insisted on this scandalous arrangement.

He already hated himself for breaking his resolve where she was concerned, and he wouldn't add fuel to his shame.

The fire burned in the hearth, and after shedding her cloak, she went immediately to it, rubbing her hands before the flame.

"It's rather a cool night for summer," she said, rubbing her arms now. "I should think we would have a little more warmth left in the season." She turned, a smile on her lips.

In the presence of her beauty, he'd forgotten to hide his torment, and it must have shown on his face because her smile faded as she took him in.

"Something's wrong," she said, turning fully to him.

She wore a gown of the purest lilac, and with her golden coloring, she looked as though she had stepped from some kind of fairy tale or Nordic myth perhaps. Whichever it was, she was not of this world with the fire illuminating her from behind.

It was better if he got this over with quickly, so he spoke directly. "I must leave for Stonegate Manor in the morning."

Her eyes pinched with sudden pain. "It's not your grand-mother, is it?"

He hated how her concern immediately went to his grandmother like that, how worried she was that something might have happened to her when really he intended to end their love affair.

He was a coward as well as a scoundrel it seemed.

"My grandmother is quite well. Her letters have been filled with the news of the village all summer. It seems there's a new organist at the church causing quite a stir." He pushed his hand through his hair. "No, I'm afraid the estate requires my attention."

This was not a lie, but it felt like one. He'd neglected his farmers for much of the growing season, relying on his steward to manage any issues that arose. He didn't like to leave such matters to hired hands, preferring to make himself available to his tenants. But he hadn't planned on starting a love affair with the woman he had loved all his life.

A line appeared between her brows. "Oh, I'm sorry to hear that. I'm sure it will only take a few days. Stonegate Manor is hardly a day's ride from London. You'll be back by next week, and we'll celebrate your birthday then."

He tried not to flinch at the mention of his birthday. She picked up the book they had been reading together, a novel by an anonymous author, and traced the leather cover. It was a story of pride and misunderstanding, and the characters were quite compelling. But what they read seemed not to matter to Caroline. She would lie for hours with her head in his lap, listening to the sound of his voice, and he'd never been happier in all of his life.

That was why it was so difficult to get the next words out. "I'm afraid I won't be returning to London."

He hoped that would be enough. He hoped she wouldn't make him say the words because he knew he wouldn't be able to. It would be a lie if he told her their affair was over because in his heart it never would be. He would always love her.

That was what this was for him.

Love.

And that was why he had to end it.

She set down the book carefully, her fingers still on its cover. "I see," she said, and he watched her as if she were physically gathering her strength. "I suppose our arrangement has reached its natural conclusion then."

The words pierced him like a dagger, his heart thudding as though it would break from his chest.

"I suppose it has."

She had spoken the words so calmly, and it left an eerie sensation trailing over his skin. He had expected theatrics, hysterics, sobbing, and yelling. But had he been thinking, he would have known there would be none of those. Not with Caroline. He remembered what she had told him that day about her mother, and he understood now the demons that haunted her, that kept her in tight control of her emotions and her world. She wouldn't lose that now when she needed to maintain control. He understood that.

She turned, reaching for her cloak.

Something unrelenting gripped him, and he wondered if it would rob him completely of air.

"You don't need to go." He reached for her hand, stilling it on the fabric of her cloak. "Stay. Stay the night. One last time."

When she looked up, he swore her eyes were glistening more than they had been. Or was it a trick of the light?

Her smile was soft and far too knowing for someone so young. He had done that to her. He had made her like that. Wary at too early an age.

But no, it wasn't him. Something had made her this way before, and his actions only compounded her understanding.

"I'm not sure that would be a good idea." She laid a hand against his chest. "I think it would be best if we just said goodbye now. It will be so much harder in the morning."

He thought her voice might have cracked the smallest bit at the end, but she was doing an incredible job of keeping herself together, and he wondered at that. She had claimed to want nothing more than something physical, and yet she was clearly unsettled by his news.

He wasn't sure it would be easier to say goodbye at any

time, but he would be as strong as she was pretending to be. He bent and kissed her cheek, lingering just a moment longer to remember her scent, to capture it long enough to last a lifetime, however short that lifetime might be.

She hesitated before stepping back and out of his arms. She gathered her cloak and turned to the door. He moved to follow her, but she stopped him.

"I know my way down. I'll be sure I'm not seen." She gave him one last smile, timid and wobbly, and she turned to the door.

For one insane moment, he wanted to stop her. He wanted to pull her back into his arms and tell her never to leave. To marry him. To grow old with him.

But that was a luxury he did not have.

Curiously it was she who stopped. She who turned back to him.

Her chin was steady now as she faced him. "Hawk, I owe you an apology. I misjudged you, and I laid blame at your feet that you didn't deserve. I'm sorry for that. I'm sorry that I wasted so much time thinking you were a person you weren't. I know better now. You're remarkable really, and Philip is lucky to have you for his friend."

He was left without words, and it was as though the world about him was rearranging itself. A new normal settled like a tangible thing between them, and he realized for the first time they were no longer enemies. Peace was what he felt, but it was tinged with sadness and despair at what was to come. Or rather not come.

"Thank you," he finally managed. "But I think Philip is even luckier to have you for a sister. It's not all little sisters who go to such lengths to avenge their brother's honor." He tried to smile, but he couldn't force the muscles of his face to move in a way he did not feel.

When she laughed the sound was brittle and shallow. "I think Philip would have a different outlook on what it was I was trying to do for him."

He tilted his head. "I'm sure deep down he understands."

There was an expectant pause then, and he felt compelled to fill it.

"Caroline, about Lady Winnaretta..."

She held up a hand, cutting him off. Her expression was one of quiet acceptance. "I don't need to know the truth, Hawk. Not anymore. What happened between Lady Winnaretta and Philip is their concern alone. I know now what Philip must have felt, and why he did what he did. I no longer blame anyone for their actions during that time."

Something real and solid shifted inside of him. He thought he would feel lighter at her words, but it wasn't that. It was as though he had thought the burden he had been carrying would be the one to change everything if only she gave him permission to release it. Only now she had, and he didn't feel any better.

Because it wasn't old scars that stood between them now. Their relationship had changed the moment he kissed her, and it was no longer enough to clear the battlefield of the past. Now it was the future that was standing between them.

She didn't want a husband, and he couldn't give her one.

It wasn't until then that his heart broke as the reality of their situation descended on him in perfect clarity.

"Goodbye, Caroline," he said.

Her smile was soft. "Goodbye, Hawk."

When the door closed softly behind her, he sank right where he stood. His legs gave out, and he hit the floor with a thud, burying his face in his hands. He shut his eyes, tight, and willed the darkness that hung before him to part like a curtain, letting him see beyond it. Beyond his thirtieth birthday and the coming end.

He wanted to see a future with Caroline. He wanted to see a future with the family they made. He wanted that brief moment when he had stood in her arms after the first time he made love to her to come back to him.

But no matter how hard he tried, all he saw was the coming darkness.

12

She was prepared for Audrey, and she was equally prepared to tell her cousin to go away as nicely and lovingly as possible.

She was not, however, prepared for Philip.

She'd retreated to her garden folly, closing the door between her and the rest of the world.

The thing about it was she wasn't upset. She wasn't even sad.

She was devastated, and she hated herself for it.

It was as though she couldn't be expected to continue functioning now. How could she? Everything in her life that had meaning of late was suddenly gone.

What was worse, it was an arrangement of her making. This was what she had purported to want. Nothing emotional. Just an agreement between two people who found one another attractive for mutual physical gratification.

So why did she feel so bereft as though everything had been stripped away from her?

She had tried to be strong, but that only resulted in her

wandering about Mattingly House as if she'd never been there before, touching railings and framed portraits as if she were seeing them for the first time.

What a nutter.

She'd fled to the garden when her mother had emerged in one of her rare appearances outside her bedchamber to inquire if Caroline thought she might wed this season. Her mother had done this periodically throughout the last three seasons Caroline had been out, but it never before needled her the way it just did.

Because she suddenly very much wished to marry, except the gentleman she wished to marry had no designs on her in that way.

He was leaving for Stonegate Manor.

She hadn't even asked him why. Of course he had explained it as estate business, but she was wise enough to know that estate business was just a gentleman's way of hiding all kinds of misdeeds.

She'd given herself a mental shake for that one. She knew better than to disparage Hawk's character now. In fact, she was fairly certain the man did not have a single ignoble bone in his body. Damn him.

So why was he ending their relationship?

It had seemed so abrupt, but then it wasn't as though she had begun this affair with an end date in mind. Perhaps she had unconsciously thought they would carry on as they were until the end of the season. But there was still more than a month left.

So, what had happened? Was he using estate business as an excuse to end things with her? Was he not happy?

This thought gave her pause. He always seemed to enjoy their time together. He'd even seemed eager. She still flushed at the memories of the things they had done. If nothing else, she had gotten what she wished for when it came to the physical act. It was only that she had discovered she wanted so much more.

She lay on the cushions, her legs sprawled across the thick carpet as she looked through the glass at the night sky. It was still early, but she watched as each of the stars appeared in the sky as if she could see each one light like a candle touched by flame.

When she heard the door of the folly open, she already had her excuse on her lips for Audrey, but she was startled when she heard Philip's voice.

"You'll get an ache in your neck lying like that."

She sat up so quickly she feared she would get an ache in her neck but for entirely different reasons.

"Philip. Whatever are you doing here? Shouldn't you be out?"

He raised an eyebrow. "Shouldn't you?"

She pulled her knees up and wrapped her arms around her legs. "I don't think there's much point in it to be honest."

He walked over to her and dropped to the floor beside her, knocking his shoulder into hers.

"I somehow knew you were going to say that." He propped the cushions behind him and leaned back against the wall, settling in. "Care to tell me why you think that?"

She wrinkled her nose. "Absolutely not."

He laughed, the sound soft and warm in the small space. "You always were stubborn."

She leaned back to get a better look at him. "I am not stubborn in the least."

"You would say that just to be stubborn."

She pressed her lips together in stubborn silence, which only made Philip laugh more. She enjoyed the sound of it, hearing such mirth from him. It made her realize how much

Philip hadn't laughed in the last few years, and it suddenly occurred to her how he had changed since his broken engagement.

"Perhaps I'll tell you if you tell me," she offered, knowing the risk she was taking.

Could she tell him about Hawk? Part of her feared Philip would call the man out for ruining his sister, but somehow, she didn't think he would. He might insist they marry though, and that seemed like such an impossibility now.

He raised that eyebrow again at this. "Can I really trust you to tell me? I have a feeling whatever it is that plagues you is something far more scandalous than my broken engagement, which has grown rather stale over the past five years."

He was right, of course. A broken engagement that occurred five years previously was dead to the gossips of the *ton*. But what Caroline had done—that was enough to ruin the entire family forever.

"I will tell you enough that you may help me. What do you say to that?"

He seemed to consider this, tilting his head dramatically to one side. "All right." He pushed himself to a more upright position. "I was actually in love with Lady Winnaretta when she broke off our engagement. What is your excuse?"

She forgot entirely what she had been prepared to say, something vague and cloaked in nuance to avoid Philip's suspicion, but at his pronouncement, she forgot words completely.

"You were?" she blurted, surprise driving her speech.

Philip nodded succinctly. "Madly in love I would say. I was already picturing the life we would have together when the baby was born." He paused as if deciding how much to say, and she wasn't surprised when he added, "Even though the baby wasn't mine."

Somehow she had known. Over the past few weeks, she had sensed something wasn't right about the picture Philip and Winnie had painted of their circumstances, but the truth was far sadder. Caroline reached out a hand involuntarily, gripping Philip's compulsively. "I'm so sorry. I didn't know..."

"No, you didn't. And yet you've condemned Hawk for what happened for years. Why is that? Did you not know Winnie had asked for his help first?"

She let go of Philip's arm, wrapping her arms back around her legs as pain shot through her. Winnie had asked Hawk to marry her? But he hadn't. Curiosity and suspicion grew inside of her.

"I needed someone to blame," she said before she even knew what she was going to say, but as soon as she said it, she realized how true it was. She met Philip's gaze. "You had nearly ruined the family, and I knew you would never do that on purpose. I needed someone to be responsible, so I could understand what happened."

"You never thought I was simply in love?"

She cringed. "At the time I didn't believe in love, or rather I thought it to be something ill-advised with deleterious effects."

He laughed, the sound strained with incredulity. "That's a rather morose way of viewing things, Caroline. What would drive you to such a world view?"

She shrugged and looked away, not wanting him to see what might be in her expression. But he leaned forward, and taking her chin in his hand, brought her face back to his.

"Caroline, what happened while I was away at school?"

His eyes were warm and pleading, but she had spent so long trying to keep the truth from him, the truth of what she had seen.

She swallowed, feeling the past like a piece of bread stuck in her throat. Perhaps it was the closeness of the folly, the press of night through the windows, but something inside of her signaled it was safe to tell the secret she had held for so long.

"I was there when Mother first discovered Father's infidelities." She paused, rethought her words. "Well, then it had been his first one. You know how madly our mother loved our father when we were young. You recall how they were with each other?"

Philip shook his head. "I remember how much Mother adored Father, but I always remember Father being somewhat removed."

Philip's voice was earnest, and it made Caroline pause, searching through her memories. After several seconds, she said, "I suppose you are right. I had always thought them to be in love with one another, but I don't think that's quite right. I think it was always one-sided."

Philip nodded. "Does that change how you feel about what you saw?"

Caroline blinked as if it would help her see that night more clearly. Her mother's face angry with tears. Her father coolly reserved and distant. Suddenly it was as though someone opened the curtains and sunshine poured in on the scene, and she was seeing it for the first time.

"Mother was so upset. It was almost as if learning of Father's unfaithfulness might kill her." Caroline shook her head. "But I don't think that's all of it. I've always looked at it from her view, but that's rather unfair, isn't it?"

Philip nodded slowly. "You know how suffocating Mother can be. She means well, but—"

"Do you think she made Father unhappy?"

Philip released a deep sigh and ran a hand through his hair. "I don't think Father has ever been happy," he finally said, his voice soft as if their father's happiness was a subject that exhausted him.

Caroline never had much interaction with their father when they were young beyond the odd, doting trinket, and she thought Philip, being the son, may have been privy to more of their father's inclinations than she had been.

She leaned back against the cushions, settling into their conversation. "Philip, do you think Mother is to blame for how much it shattered her to learn of Father's affairs?"

Philip was quick to shake his head. "I don't think it's that at all. I think sometimes the people we love do things we don't expect them to, and it hurts us."

At his words, something fell inside of her like a boulder that had been perched on the edge of a rocky cliff suddenly breaking free, sliding down the hillside only to splinter in a thunderous crash.

"Philip, how did Hawk's parents die?"

Philip looked at her sharply. "You don't know?"

She shook her head, biting her lip with sudden anticipation, knowing she should have been brave enough to ask that day.

"It was a carriage accident. They were in London so his father could see to some business when they received word that Hawk had taken ill. They were racing back to Surrey when it happened."

She sucked in a breath, her world expanding to infinite possibilities with nothing more than a change in perspective.

"How is it that I never knew that?"

Philip shrugged. "Hawk never talks about it. I think it's painful for him."

"But he had Lady Sherrill to care for him." She remembered how he spoke of his grandmother. It was almost as if he had no memory of his parents at all, but perhaps that wasn't it.

Philip nodded. "That's true, but unlike us, Hawk had a close relationship with his father. He was the only child, after all, and he was expected to inherit one day. Even in the brief time they knew each other, I think a true bond formed."

She poked around in what Philip had told her, trying to find the answer to Hawk's reluctance to marry, his sudden decision to end their affair, but it was as though she were still missing one crucial piece.

She met Philip's gaze, licked her lips. "Philip, Hawk said something about how it was Lady Winnaretta's secret. About what happened with your broken engagement. Is that true?"

Philip's expression darkened, and for a moment, she thought he wouldn't answer, but then he said, "Yes, it is. Why?"

She pushed to her feet, tripping once on her skirts. "I must speak with Lady Winnaretta."

Philip all but flew to his feet, grabbing her shoulders in a fierce grip. "You can't, Caroline. I don't care what good you think you're doing—"

Caroline cut off his flow of words by grasping the lapels of his jacket in a firm grip and giving him a shake. "Believe it or not, Philip, this is not about you. I need to speak with her for other reasons."

It was likely the shock of her words that had him

releasing her, and she was nearly to the door when Philip called after her. "Then who is this about?"

She turned back to him, determination settling on her features. "It's about the man I love," she said and disappeared into the darkness.

∽

"You will not speak with the lady."

"But I must."

Caroline would not back down no matter how intimidating the beast of a woman who stood before her was. She had introduced herself with a rough bark as only Mathilda, and with a succinct nod had informed Caroline that she would not speak to Lady Winnaretta.

Except Caroline couldn't *not* speak to her. Lady Winnaretta was the only one who could give her the answers she needed.

She had shown up without notice on Lady Winnaretta's doorstep, hoping her station alone would gain her entrance. She hadn't counted on the lady having a bodyguard.

Mathilda sucked in a breath, drawing her chin a full two inches higher. "You will not." She enunciated each word as if firing the ball from a musket.

Caroline crossed her arms under her bosom. "That's unfortunate then because I shall." She backed up and sat on the chair facing the door of the small drawing room she had been shown to when she'd first knocked on the front door of Lowe Place. "And I'm not leaving until I do."

Mathilda laughed then, a horrible harsh sound that suggested painful delight. Caroline watched this opponent she hadn't anticipated, but she was oddly devoid of fear of the strange woman. Because quite simply Caroline had no other choice. She must speak with Lady Winnaretta.

Then the oddest thing happened. Mathilda unbuttoned the sleeves of her utilitarian gown and began methodically rolling back each until her rippling forearms were exposed.

Now Caroline felt a lick of fear, and it froze her to the chair. Surely this woman wouldn't intentionally harm her. Would she?

She waited as the woman adjusted the tight bun of her hair at the nape of her neck and then with slow, ponderous steps, advanced.

She didn't wait for the woman to reach the chair where Caroline still sat. Carefully she slipped her toes out from under her gown, finding the legs of the chair and wrapping her feet around them as she had done that day at Audrey's wedding breakfast. She did the same with her arms through the intricately carved arms of the chair.

When Mathilda reached her, she did exactly as Caroline predicted.

She attempted to pick her up.

But Caroline was ready and when she picked her up, the chair came with her.

Mathilda stumbled, clearly not expecting the unwieldy bulk of the chair that upset her balance. She caught herself but not before they tipped dangerously to the side, and Caroline's arm smashed into the back of a sofa. Pain radiated through her arm, but she gritted her teeth, refusing to let go.

Turning awkwardly Mathilda lumbered in the direction of the door, and Caroline realized with a sickening jolt what the woman planned to do. She would set Caroline straight outside the front door, chair and all, and she would never get to speak with Lady Winnaretta.

In a panic, Caroline began to scream. "Winnie! Winnie! You must speak to me. I need to know about Hawk." Her voice rang against the marble tiles of the foyer with ear-splitting intensity, but then it all suddenly stopped.

Mathilda slumped into her as their progress arrested in mid-air.

The chair was stuck in the doorway of the drawing room.

Caroline wasn't sure who was more surprised. Mathilda studied the doorframe like it was betraying her while Caroline tried to surmise how precarious her position was. The intricately bowed wings of the chair had become wedged in the door, and wood groaned ominously. Caroline met Mathilda's eyes just as Mathilda let go of her.

Caroline sucked in a breath and pinched her eyes against the inevitable fall, but it never came. Instead the wood continued to groan; the chair started to shift.

And then a voice called over all of it. "What about Hawk?"

Caroline couldn't stop herself. She turned her head swiftly to find Lady Winnaretta on the stairs behind her in the foyer.

"Winnie!" Caroline exclaimed. "You must help me. It's about Hawk."

The wood gave way at just that moment, the door frame splintering as the chair fell on one side. And then it stopped as it caught again farther down the jamb.

"Mathilda, help the lady down."

Caroline's grip on the chair had become desperate rather than determined and when Mathilda reached for her, wrapping her beefy arms around Caroline's slender waist, Caroline gave herself up to the woman. She was lifted bodily and set on the floor of the drawing room before

Mathilda turned and pried the chair loose. Wood splintered as the chair buckled, and Mathilda tossed it aside.

When Caroline looked to the door again, Lady Winnaretta filled it, her hands folded softly in front of her as though such things occurred in her presence every day. Caroline had forgotten how eerily beautiful the woman was, and how much it always seemed like she should be drifting through a field of wildflowers. No wonder Philip had been in love with her.

"Is Hawk in trouble?" While Winnie looked much the same as she had five years ago, her features had softened with time. She looked like a woman now instead of a child. Her rich brown hair was plaited softly about her face, giving her a serene appearance.

Caroline shifted her eyes to Mathilda, wondering if this hulk of a woman had achieved such delicate work.

"I'm not sure," Caroline finally said. "I was hoping you could help me to determine whether or not he is."

Winnie's face didn't change, but she shifted her eyes to Mathilda. She spoke then, and Caroline could not make out what she said. It sounded Scandinavian. Perhaps Norwegian? Whatever it was, Winnie had a command of the language that even Caroline could sense as she never stumbled over her words, her gaze direct on Mathilda.

The servant gave a sharp nod and left the room, closing the door behind her, which didn't quite shut against the broken frame.

"Please." Winnie gestured to the sofa Caroline had recently been pressed into.

She grimaced. "I'd rather stand if you don't mind. I shouldn't like to take too much of your time."

Winnie raised her eyebrows at this. "Really? I would think you have many questions."

"I do, but it's not for me to ask them. I've come to under-stand that now. Your secrets are yours alone, and as curious as I am to know them, it's no excuse to pry into your past."

"Even though you accuse me of nearly ruining your brother?"

Caroline's lips parted, but she was unable to speak.

Winnie's smile was knowing. "I hear things, you know, even if I do not mingle in society so much these days." She paced across the room, her hands held at the small of her back. She turned once she reached the windows on the other side. "So, what is it that you wish to know if it's not my secrets?"

"I want to know why Hawk refused to marry you when you found yourself with child."

Caroline had clearly surprised her. Her mouth tightened just the slightest of degrees, and Caroline sensed this was the greatest reaction the woman had ever given in her life. Caroline tried for a moment to remember back to five years earlier when she'd first met Lady Winnaretta Lowe. Caroline had been young and impressionable, and she had thought Winnie a proper vixen. But standing there now, facing her in this tame drawing room, Winnie appeared as nothing more than the refined lady, the proper daughter of a titled gentleman. Caroline may have even called her a friend if circumstances were different.

"Why is it that you must know?"

Caroline swallowed and prepared herself to speak because this would be it. There would be no turning back from here. But no, that wasn't right. There had been no turning back from the moment she realized she was in love with the man.

"Because I must know why he refuses to wed if I'm to convince him to marry me."

If Caroline had surprised her before, she clearly upset her now as the woman sucked in a breath.

"You wish to marry Hawk."

"Yes," Caroline said, although it hadn't been a question.

Winnie took a step toward her, stopped, a hand on the back of the sofa between them. "But...why?"

"Because I love him." The words came dangerously and easily to her lips.

Caroline held her breath. It was all she could do to contain the energy that vibrated through her, waiting for Winnie to speak. To give her the answer to all of her troubles.

But Winnie seemed to be holding her breath too as though she were deciding what to say. Finally she closed her eyes, a small smile coming to her lips, a smile so sad and world-weary it squeezed Caroline's heart.

When Winnie opened her eyes, they were wet with unshed tears. "I was in love once," she said. "I was in love with a boy who grew up on the estate neighboring ours. He was to leave for the war, and foolishly we decided to consummate our love." She laughed but the sound was full of tears. "We were young and stupid. We thought the war would be short, and he would be home before summer's end, and then we would wed. It needn't matter if he got me with child. We would be married before it was of concern." Winnie pressed the back of her hand to her mouth, her lips wavering on a silent sob, but she gathered herself.

Caroline took a short step forward, her hands suspended uselessly in front of her. "Winnie, you mustn't. I don't want you to—"

Winnie shook her head and dropped her hand. "But you must know. Because it's the only way for you to understand Hawk." She smiled now, but it caused a tear to fall from her right eye. "I found myself with child on the day I received the news that my lover had been killed." Her voice had gone cruelly cold. "I sent word to Hawk first, terrified that my father would discover what I had done and make me—"

She didn't need to finish the sentence. Caroline knew only too well how unwanted babies were dealt with. She waited as Winnie gathered herself once again.

"Hawk refused me as you know, but it didn't matter because Philip offered to marry me." Her voice broke on the last words, but she stopped herself as she harshly cleared her throat.

Caroline hadn't known. She had been young and stupid too, and she had cast blame on so many people whose only fault was being in love.

"I lost the baby," Winnie whispered, her voice suddenly without strength. "I lost the baby, and it was—" Her voice broke again, and again she cleared her throat as if forcing herself to accept the truth.

But Caroline didn't need to hear it. She knew what that baby had meant. It was the last thing Winnie had of her lost love. Without the baby, she lost everything she had once loved.

Winnie had faced a future she hadn't planned for, and Philip was there by her side.

Caroline felt a stab of guilt so great she sucked in a breath. She had been so wrong about so many things. But still—

"Winnie, darling." She took a step forward, the need to help pulsing through her. "You still haven't explained why Hawk refused to wed."

Winnie blinked, unshed tears clinging to her eyelashes. She shook her head as though she were only speaking of the obvious. "It's his father, of course. Hawk believes he won't live past his thirtieth birthday because his father didn't."

Cold, an icy and complete cold, spread through Caroline limb by limb, and she knew it would soon seize her heart if she didn't move. She reached out and clung to Winnie before letting the woman go just as abruptly. She was already to the door when Winnie cried out.

"Caroline, your brother—" Her words stopped as she choked painfully. "Your brother stood by me, and I...I treated him terribly."

Caroline somehow knew that was not what she had meant to say. She knew by the anguish writ across Winnie's face that the day she had broken her engagement she had lost both her past and her future. Caroline knew because right then she was teetering on the same brink.

Only she refused to let her future slip away from her.

"It's not too late, Winnie," she said, her voice soft and coaxing.

Winnie's eyes grew wide, and it was as if the last of the tears refused to fall.

"It's not too late," Caroline repeated and left.

13

Hawk sat in near darkness in his study at Stonegate Manor.

It was raining. He could hear the water attacking the windows, the glass panes shuddering in the wind. But though he heard it, he could not understand it. His mind was already in turmoil and could not give room to the conditions around him.

So it was that it had grown dark about him, the light falling into dusk until the day had melted into night. It had already been gloomy, and he might have used that as an excuse for not noticing when the light left, but that was all it would have been. An excuse.

In fact, he liked the darkness. He liked not being able to see beyond the small hemisphere the fire cast about the chair he had pulled dangerously close to the hearth. He hadn't wanted to sit in the middle of the room where the chairs were scattered. It suddenly felt lonely and exposed, and he wanted the comfort of the fire.

But that was all. He'd had neither drink nor food for all of the day, and he didn't really care. He could only sit there, watching the flames and wondering when it would end.

He realized he was waiting for the clock to chime in the corridor, for its ominous tones to cry out the midnight hour. He didn't know why, but he had decided upon this as the moment everything would end. When the clock would strike midnight on his thirtieth birthday. For surely that was when it would happen. It had a proper weight to it, a seriousness that would suggest such a change.

He listened now to only the crackle of the fire, the steady beat of his own heart, and the hourly chiming of the clock. He had just counted eight chimes, and he knew within hours he would no longer need to suffer.

He would no longer need to suffer at the memory of her walking through the door one final time. He would no longer need to suffer at the memory of her in his arms, her scent of roses and the crackle of her golden hair. The way her eyelashes fanned her cheeks when she slept, the way she could so perfectly curl her body against his.

He wanted the end to come now. He wanted it simply to be over. He never should have started the affair in the first place. He knew better, and yet he had fallen victim to a love that he had harbored for so long, and once offered to him, he could no longer resist it.

But did he truly wish he had not done it? Or was that only the exquisite pain talking now? The pain of having let her go.

The wind outside turned baleful, slapping against the windowpanes with renewed vigor, and dimly he turned in the direction of the windows, curtained for the night against the cold. But even as he stared at them, he realized the banging was not coming from the windows.

It was coming from somewhere deeper in the house.

His grandmother had gone to the next village over to visit with a friend, and he was alone at Stonegate Manor except for the servants. But he'd given them the evening off. Whatever was the source of the banging it was not human. It couldn't be.

He rose, overcome not with a sense of fear but rather a sense of curiosity. Was this how it would come? The end would be heralded by a spectral noise?

He opened the door to the corridor, and the soft light of a lamp there hurt his eyes. He wondered which servant had been kind enough to leave the light, but his thoughts were soon interrupted by the incessant banging, which had grown louder now. He stepped into the corridor, the door to the study left absently ajar, and he wandered in the direction of the noise.

He had made it nearly to the front of the house when he realized someone was banging on the front door. He quickened his steps, hurrying the last several yards as fear niggled its way through his senses. If someone were at the door at this hour in the dark of a stormy night, something must be terribly wrong.

He reached the foyer and without stopping, wrenched open the front door. He didn't understand what happened then. A small, cloak-wrapped bundle spilled inside, and he caught it against his chest. It was whoever had been banging, but although he had opened the door, the person's small fists continued their assault, only now it was against his chest.

"Please, please, I must speak with the earl." The voice was muffled under the folds of the sodden cloak, but it needn't matter because his mind had just connected the shape of the bundle with a memory, and his arms tightened instinctively.

"Caroline," he breathed, his hands scrambling to push back the hood of the garment.

He had to see her face; he was desperate to see it. It was as though until he could see the blue of her eyes, he couldn't know for sure she was all right.

"Caroline, what's happened?" He pushed the last fold of the hood aside at the same time she looked up, and he watched the realization dawn on her face.

"Hawk." He had never heard his name spoken like that. As if she needed to say it like she needed to breathe. "Hawk, don't do it. Please. There's another way. I promise. We'll figure it out together."

Her hands searched the front of his jacket, and he wasn't sure what she was doing until her arms popped free of her heavy, drenched cloak, and she latched onto him. Her gloved hands were just as sodden, and finally it penetrated his confused senses that she was shivering. Badly.

"Hawk, please. You must listen to me. I spoke to Winnie. I know what happened. It doesn't matter—"

She spoke to Winnie?

His mind was more clouded than ever, but through it came one startling truth.

He had to get her warm.

She was still chattering when he scooped her up, and memories of that day at the house party coursed through him. He didn't take her upstairs this time. He headed directly for his study and likely the only burning fire in the manor that night.

He cursed himself for being a fool and giving the staff the night off. He needed to get her warm and probably fed. How long had she been standing on his doorstep? Had she come from London in this storm?

He strode through the study door, kicking it shut behind

him to try to keep the warmth in the room. He set her on her feet, and this time, he didn't need to ask her to strip. He did it for her, his hands moving in familiar patterns. The cloak, her gown, her chemise, her corset, her stockings. He rummaged in the trunk in the corner and withdraw the quilts his grandmother kept there for winter nights when she liked to sew by the fire.

The entire time Caroline spoke through trembling lips, and he only caught individual words.

Winnie.

The baby.

His father.

His father?

What had Winnie told her?

He spread the quilts in front of the fire, grabbed the cushions from the sofa, and finally forced Caroline into the cocoon he had created. She went, unresisting, her words unceasing. He added wood to the fire, stoking it until the flames roared in the fireplace, and only then did he stand and shuck his own, now sodden clothes. As he slipped under the quilts, pulled Caroline's frigid body against his, she never once stopped speaking.

He pulled her into his arms and tucked her head under his chin, and only then did he place a single finger over her lips.

"Pet, you must speak more slowly and with a great deal more sense. First, what are you doing here?"

She leaned back to look up at him, her head on the cushion next to his now. "I've come to stop you from killing yourself."

"Killing myself?" The shock of her words rippled through him. "Why would you think I was going to kill myself?"

"Winnie told me," she said. "She said you didn't expect to live past your thirtieth birthday. That's tomorrow, and I knew suddenly why you said you must go to Stonegate Manor. Hawk, please—" She gripped his cheek in her icy fingers, but he curled his much warmer hand over hers.

"Caroline, I have no plans to end my life." He spoke the words quietly and with a heavy degree of reason.

She blinked as though trying to see things in a suddenly different light. "You don't?"

He shook his head, shifting so he could face her. "Absolutely not. You mustn't vex yourself so." They faced each other, nestled under the blankets, and he took her hands into one of his, pressed them against his chest to try to relay some heat into them while he moved his free hand up and down her back in lingering strokes.

"Then why are you here?" She breathed the question.

"I already asked you that question, and I do not have nearly all of the story."

She licked her lips. "There isn't much to tell."

"I think there's a great deal to tell. The first being how you spoke to Winnie. She's carefully guarded as I understand."

She blinked. "Do you mean that wretched woman, Mathilda?"

"That's the one."

She shook her head as if batting away a pesky fly. "She was no matter. You more than anyone should know how determined I am once I set my mind on something."

He couldn't help but stare. "You faced Mathilda...and succeeded?"

"Of course I did." She moved her hands, encasing his with her own now. "Hawk, you must know how important you are to me." She hesitated, as if deciding whether or not to say more. But then she said, "I love you, Hawk. I couldn't let you do whatever it was you had planned."

Her words coursed through him like the heat of a fine liquor, and he warmed from the inside out. But—

"Caroline, you're overwrought. You don't mean that."

"Don't tell me what I mean, Hawkins Savage. I know perfectly well what I feel, and you will just need to live with that."

He shuddered under her determination but more under the meaning of her words. He hadn't forgotten the chiming of the clock and listened now, waiting for its toll.

But Caroline continued to speak. "Winnie told me everything. About how you refused to marry her when she found herself with child, and she told me the reason you gave. But what she didn't tell me was why." She reached up, cupped his cheek again, and he was relieved to feel warmth in her fingers. "Why, Hawk? Why do you believe your life is going to end? Why can't you see your own future?"

He wanted to tell her it was nothing. He wanted to dismiss her concerns. But in the back of his mind, the count-down continued. Any moment now there would be nine chimes from the clock, and he would be that much closer to the end.

But he didn't want it to end now. Caroline loved him. She had come back to him. She had come to save him. But she couldn't. Nothing could save him.

"Oh pet, I'm sorry. It simply must be this way. I can't...I can't..." But he couldn't find the words to explain it to her. He didn't know how to tell her about the black thing he had been carrying since that day his parents died.

He tried, he really tried, but every time he thought he gathered the words his tongue grew thick and unwieldy.

And yet she continued to watch him, her eyes so hopeful and expectant, as though she truly believed he could.

It hurt. It hurt deeply, and he hated himself with a sudden ferocity. He wanted to give her this. The truth. She deserved so very much more.

But every time he pushed at it, the future never gave him answers.

"I don't know," he finally said, hating himself for the weakness of his words. "I can't see my future, Caroline. I can't see my future past now."

Her eyes searched him, her gaze prodding for more, but he had nothing left to give. She took the hand she cradled between her own and moved it to rest on the soft swell of her belly.

"But your future is already here, Hawk." She swallowed and pressed his hand more tightly against her. "Your future is here because I'm carrying your child."

SHE HADN'T MEANT to tell him. Not like this.

She had wanted it to be a welcomed surprise and not a catalyst for forcing him to see their future together.

To force him to marry her.

While that was what she wanted, she would never force him to it. He had to decide on his own.

For the first time she realized she might not be successful at this. She still didn't understand why it was he thought his life would stop when his father's had, and somehow without that knowledge she felt powerless to help him, and it frightened her.

So, she had done what had been in her power to do. She had told of the baby she suspected she was carrying. While she couldn't be certain until a doctor examined her, she now felt she had enough clues to be confident in her announcement.

She watched Hawk's face carefully, waiting for the realization to sink in. But his face never changed. He kept his gaze locked on hers, his hand still against her belly. She waited, her breathing shallow, hoping for him to say something that might make it all better.

"You can't be carrying my child," he finally whispered, and her heart broke into a thousand pieces.

"But I am, Hawk. I am carrying your child." She pressed his hand more firmly to her, willing him to understand.

And that was when she saw it. The wetness that had gathered at the corners of his eyes, the slight strain at the corners of his lips.

He was doing everything he could to hold himself back, to keep contained the well of emotion so obviously brimming to the fore within him.

She took his face in both of her hands. "Hawk, I love you. I'm carrying your child, and I want to marry you. Those are the facts. Do you understand that? No matter how you feel now or what you think may happen, those are your feelings. And feelings are not always aligned with the facts. Trust me, love. You should know how capable I am of twisting the facts to suit my emotions." Her tone had taken on a pleading note, and she hoped honesty would work where truth hadn't.

"You can't, Caroline. You can't be carrying my child."

"I am," she said, and now there were tears in her voice. Tears for him and for her. They carried so many scars inflicted upon them by the ones they loved through no fault of anyone. And yet here they were. Clinging to each other for hope and a future. "Hawk, please. Tell me what happened. Tell me so I can help."

He shook his head, and tears dislodged from the corners of his eyes. "I can't. I can't...figure out what it is inside of me."

She felt the resistance in him shift as if it were a tangible thing. "What is it, Hawk? What is inside of you?"

He wrenched his hand free and rolled onto his back, pressing his fingers into his chest above his heart. "I can't make the blackness go away. I can't see past it. My father... died. He died before he turned thirty. I can't possibly..."

She came up on her elbow and leaned over him, tugging his fingers from his chest, seeing the red indentations he had left there. "Tell me about the blackness, Hawk. Tell me what makes it come."

He closed his eyes, but she wanted him to look at her. She wanted to see his emotions in his eyes, but it was as though he couldn't speak without closing them, so she let him.

"I didn't know they had sent for my parents. My nanny and the housekeeper. They sent word to London that I was ill. I don't remember feeling that poorly, but they wanted my parents to know." He shook his head back and forth against the pillow. "They started back. They started back for me, but the roads....it had snowed. It was icy. It was dark. It was so dark." His voice had lost much of its strength, and with a squeeze of her own heart, she realized he was slipping deeper into memory, reliving that terrible time. She gripped his hand, trying to keep him with her at the same time she didn't wish to interrupt him. "They never came home," he finished with a whisper.

She wiped at the tears that fell silently from the corners of his eyes and waited, willing him to say more, but he only shook his head back and forth like a metronome against the cushion.

"Hawk." She kept her voice low. "Hawk, do you miss your parents? Is that why you see the blackness?"

He shook his head. "Grandmother was always so kind to me. She took care of me. She made sure—" But the words just stopped, his lips parted soundlessly on nothing.

Caroline sifted through her thoughts. All those nights she had spent in his arms when he had spoken of his childhood. The games he had played with Dash and Philip. The way his grandmother spoiled him with sweets and toys and baubles. There was nothing but happy memories with the exception of his parents who simply weren't there.

She swallowed, licked her lips. "Hawk, darling, is the blackness...is it guilt? Do you feel guilty for your father's death?"

His eyes pinched tightly as if he were in physical pain, and he tried to press his hand against his chest again. She held onto him, one hand cupping his thrashing head, the other trying to keep hold of the hand he tried to push into himself.

"Is it guilt, Hawk? Do you think you caused your parents' death?"

A noise had started low in his throat, a humming noise of pain and torture. But she kept going.

"Hawk, do you think if you hadn't been ill your parents would still be alive today?"

The sob broke from him in a cry of anguish, his body arching against the floor as if trying to get away from the pain. She wrapped her arms around him, covering his body with her own while the sobs wracked his body. She held him as his cries turned ragged, the tears dampened the cushion behind his head, as his body convulsed with pain.

It was several minutes before his heart slowed to a steady pace beneath her ear, before his chest rose and fell in unvarying breaths. She held him through all of it, protecting his body with her own as the pain and guilt of a scared little boy left him in comprehensive waves.

For a moment she thought he had fallen asleep, he grew so still beneath her, but then she felt his hand at the back of her head, massaging the spot where scalp met neck, and pleasure radiated through her.

"Hawk," she said tentatively, questioningly, but he didn't speak, his hand only continued to stroke and knead, and her body turned to liquid, draping across him.

His other hand began to move, sliding down her body in a stroke of heat. He cupped her, pulling ever so gently until she shifted, straddling him. She came above him, her breasts dragging achingly across the rough hair of his chest. He was already reaching for her hot center, fitted himself to her, and entered her in one fluid motion. His movements were sure, calculated, and it was as though he was searching for something.

Searching for something in the warmth of her core, in the connection of their bodies. It was primal and base and too powerful for her not to feel it.

He was finding life with her.

He hadn't moved since he'd entered her, but his hands gripped her hips, holding her in place. His eyes were still closed, his lips a thin line, but the muscles of his face had relaxed.

She started to move. Tentative and small, she shifted her hips against him. She felt him respond, a small twitch in her tight sheath, but it was as though a lightning bolt traveled through her.

She began to move with concentrated effort, her thrusts

deep as she lifted her hips higher and higher. With each movement, she drew him deeper, brought him closer, her fingers splayed in the hair on his chest, her fingers digging into the hard muscle there.

She couldn't remember closing her eyes, throwing her head back, but all at once she no longer needed to see him. She could feel him, all of him, body and soul, and the sensations that rushed through her grew deeper, more poignant, as she took him, hard, his fingers biting into her hips now.

Then he began to move, lifting up into her as she slammed down onto him, and it was though for a moment they became one. When she came it was hard, brutal, and unforgiving, but he came with her, sitting up to wrap her in his arms, to bury his face against her.

When they collapsed against the cushions, they still clung to each other, limb for limb, breath for breath. She didn't know if they dozed. Everything about them had become clouded and hazy except for the feel of each other.

It was sometime later when she felt him stiffen in her arms, and she opened her eyes, watching him expectantly. Somewhere, faintly, she heard the tolling of a clock and with each ring of the chime, a muscle in his cheek jumped until the house fell silent again.

His eyes were wide, staring unblinkingly at the ceiling. She rose up on her elbow and pressed her lips to his, shattering whatever trance he had been trapped in.

When she lifted her head, his eyes focused on her, and slowly, achingly slowly, a smile came to his lips.

"Hello, pet," he said, and just like that it was as though they were starting all over again. A newness gripped her and with it came the lightness of innocence. She knew it was a mirage. They had been through too much to feel so weightless now, but it wasn't innocence that buoyed her.

It was hope.

"Hello, love," she said and kissed him again.

His hands moved down her body, stopping to cradle her belly. His eyes never left hers, and in that moment, they were captured in a world all their own.

"I just wanted to make sure you were still here," he said. "It's midnight," he said with a shaky laugh. "I worried you might disappear at the stroke of twelve."

She gripped his hand and put all her strength into her voice. "*We* are still here."

She watched as the meaning of her words washed over him, and now his laugh was stronger. It grew, encompassing her and filling the room with a warmth the fire could never outmatch.

"Oh God, Caroline, you scared me half to death," he said, catching his breath. "Coming upon a man in the dark like that. I thought you were some kind of specter."

She couldn't stop her own smile at the relief she saw on his features. Whatever darkness that swallowed him so completely the whole of his life seemed to have broken apart, letting in the light. She knew the darkness would never go away completely. Pain like that simply couldn't. But perhaps now she could help him carry the weight of it.

They would carry the weight of it, she and all the children she would give him.

"Do you often cavort with ghosts in the darkest hour of the night?"

His eyes shone with humor. "I do not. But I'm finding I do many things I've never done before with you in my life." He cradled the side of her face, and she nestled against him, marveling in the feel of the warmth and callus of his palm.

"Thank you, pet," he said now, his voice growing soft and wondering. "Thank you for not letting me go."

She covered his hand with her own. "Sometimes those we love do things that we don't expect them to, and it can hurt us because we love them. But it doesn't mean we give up."

His eyes narrowed. "Did Audrey tell you that?"

She laughed. "Someone far wiser did actually."

His eyebrow lifted. "Is that so?"

She silenced him with a kiss. When she lifted her head, his expression had sobered.

"Thank you, Caroline." He spoke her name with heavy meaning. "Thank you for..." His voice trailed off as if he couldn't name what it was she had done. "I never realized I carried such guilt until you said it."

There was a gratefulness in his eyes that nearly broke her, and it was all she could do to wrap her arms around him and feel the beat of his heart against hers. But he eased her away from him, and the look she saw in his eyes was painful. She held her breath.

"Caroline, I want you to know that I'll take care of you and baby. You mustn't worry that I'll force you to marry me, and I promise—"

Once more she silenced him with a kiss, but it was a difficult thing to do as she couldn't stop smiling. When she finally released him, she said, "I'm very sorry to inform you, Lord Stonegate, but I've changed my mind about our affair." The pained look in his eyes had disappeared, replaced by confusion, and she went on, cupping his cheek in her hand, "You made me realize there is more to love than just the terrible things I have witnessed. You put my mind at ease and give me hope when I think there is none. I'm afraid I realized I quite simply cannot live without you. Once you told me that should you ever marry, you would only want me for a wife. Is that still true?"

The confusion disappeared from his eyes, and this time it was replaced by a warm desire so exquisite it might constrict her chest.

"It's truer now more than ever."

"In that case, I accept your proposal."

His smile was slow and playful. "I don't believe I asked."

"But I knew you would, so I thought I'd simply save you the trouble."

He kissed her then with a growl, and she forgot everything else.

It was several hours later, after they had dozed and made love again, that he nuzzled her ear. She could feel his smile against her as he said, "I still have one more question, pet."

She leaned back to look at him. "What is that?"

His expression grew pensive, and she worried the darkness was trying to reach him again. But then he asked, "However did you defeat Mathilda?"

The surprise question caused a snort of laughter to catch in her throat. "It's a funny story actually."

He settled into the cushions, cradling her in his arms. "Well, it just so happens I have all the rest of my life to hear it."

14

Some years later...

SHE HANDED him the wrapped bundle, settling back against the pillows with a sigh.

"There you are, my lord. I believe my part of the bargain has been fulfilled. You have an heir."

Hawk cradled the swaddled bundle in his arms, ignoring or perhaps not having heard her pithy comment. But it didn't matter. This was the moment she cherished most.

The wondrous look on his face whenever she placed his newborn child into his arms.

He never failed to appear surprised, as though he was just as incredulous as he had been before that he could have created something so precious, so innocent, so pure. And that expression was one she held close to her heart.

He swayed on his feet, calming the baby as he began to mewl. She watched, unspeaking as he traced his son's forehead with a single finger, the candlelight glinting off the gold band on the third finger of his left hand. First he traced the baby's round, soft cheeks, the curve of an eyebrow, and then the dimple of his little chin.

He had done exactly the same with each of the girls. It was as though he were memorizing their features, as if they may suddenly change on him one day.

And they did, routinely change that is, as children often do, but no matter what happened, he still continued to look at them with wondrous amazement.

It was several minutes before she touched his elbow, drawing his attention back to the present. She hated to do it, to break the spell that so enraptured him, this precious moment between father and son, but her breasts were heavy with milk, and she knew the babe would begin to fuss shortly.

Without a word Hawk handed his son back, and she nestled the babe against her breast as Hawk sat on the bed next to her, cradling them both in the crook of his arm.

"I knew one day you would finally get around to giving me a son," he said, his voice playfully light.

But it didn't matter if he were joking or not. To hear him speak so lightly of his future was something that always caused a burst of joy within her.

"You know perfectly well I was seeing to my own needs first. Three daughters should suffice to keep me in good company well into my doddering years."

He sucked in an offended breath. "And just where will I be in those same doddering years?"

Her smile was swift as she leaned back and kissed him. "Off carousing with your sons, of course."

His smile was slow and oozed satisfaction. "Did you say sons?" He delicately traced the downy head of the son she currently held. "Do you plan to give me more than just the one?"

"We'll see," she said, her own smile full to bursting. "We never know what the future holds, do we?"

"You've never been more right, pet," he said and kissed her.

ABOUT THE AUTHOR

Jessie decided to be a writer because there were too many lives she wanted to live to just pick one.

Taking her history degree dangerously, Jessie tells the stories of courageous heroines, the men who dared to love them, and the world that tried to defeat them.

Jessie makes her home in New Hampshire where she lives with her husband and two very opinionated Basset hounds. For more, visit her website at jessieclever.com.

Made in the USA
Columbia, SC
26 January 2022

54819763R00131